FAIR WEATHER FOUL

FAIR WEATHER FOUL

SEAN FREEMAN

William Morrow and Company, Inc., New York

Library of Congress Cataloging-in-Publication Data

Freeman, Sean.
  Fair weather foul.

  I. Title.
PS3556.R3926F35   1988   813'.54   87-24718
ISBN 0-688-07588-6

Printed in the United States of America
1 2 3 4 5 6 7 8 9 10
First Edition

BOOK DESIGN BY KARIN BATTEN

To Lynne
Drewes

No culture has yet solved the dilemma each has faced with the growth of a conscious mind: how to live a moral and compassionate existence when one is fully aware of the blood, the horror inherent in all life, when one finds darkness not only in one's own culture but within oneself. If there is a stage at which an individual life becomes truly adult, it must be when one grasps the irony in its unfolding and accepts responsibility for a life lived in the midst of such paradox.

—Barry Lopez,
Arctic Dreams

Prologue

Gloveolium.

It is my contention that Gloveolium is the cause of our sorrow, the root of all evil. Next to the spurt of semen, Gloveolium was the viscous solution more American boys had in the palms of their hands than any other. That clear oily substance, squeezed from the can into the pocket of the autographed Mickey Mantle baseball glove, was worked with adolescent ardor: kneading, rubbing, grinding, squeezing, and stroking, for hour upon hour, until the glove was dark and supple, the body limp and exhausted.

If you doubt what I say just look at who went to Vietnam! Not the tennis team, not the debate society, and certainly not the girls. Noooo! It was the Little Leaguers who went. America's boys who'd been pounding their palms with Gloveolium since the third grade.

When the anthem played we put aside our bat and glove, took up the rifle, and stood tall. Infected with Gloveolium we marched off to do battle with a country—nay, a civilization—that had never known competitive sports. Never! I mean talk about subversive-Commie-faggot behavior! No baseball, no basketball, no football, not even soccer or Ping-Pong. No wonder the limp-wrist intellectual college crowd was so sympathetic!

And no wonder baseball went into a decline in the sixties and seventies. All the long-ball hitters, big arms, and double-play combos were in the jungle stomping out the yellow horde and the Red menace, getting their legs and arms blown off (here I tap my hook against the desk).

Millions of men with the most highly sophisticated of weapons were sent to fight a bunch of Stone Age peasants, and they kicked our asses! They had something going for them that was not in the playbook. You couldn't tell their players without a scorecard, and there was no scorecard. We couldn't defense them. They hit our best pitching. They ran on us. They capitalized on our mistakes. And they had a bench that went on forever.

Gloveoliumed since childhood, America's finest lost. And not for want of trying! We had the best team money could buy, but the other guys were better. They had whatever it was that money couldn't buy: determination, dedication, destiny, a cause.

Home from the war in shame, no one wanted to hear about the big game—the one that got away. We retreated to the bedroom of a lost childhood where the walls still flew pennants, and snapshots on the desk stood like tombstones: high school graduation, a vividly forgotten girl, summers fishing in Alaska. Deep in the closet, tucked in the corner beside the pilfered license plates and the stack of nudie-cuties: a glove. Snug in the pocket, a ball protected its shape, and beside it stood a half-empty can of that old petrochemical jism Gloveolium.

But it was too late. We'd been bit by the brain-of-the-dog so long ago, and the poison was so deep within, that the glove smelled of dead water buffalo. The ball (gripped with hook and not fingers) looked suspiciously lethal, as if it were about to explode—missing as it was the spoon and pin of the hand grenade. And the *wap* of the ball as it hit the pocket echoed like incoming mortar fire.

Nothing would ever look the same again.

We were like sleepers deprived of our dreams; every time we began to doze, and the eyes to move, we were awakened. Sent to war at seventeen, eighteen, nineteen, our childhood dreams shattered by nightmares, we were old men at twenty. Bitter, cynical, seething just below the surface, we turned inward, held tight to our horrors, and lived the sleep of the disturbed.

Slowly our fans returned, but the game was never broached. Some few would probe the perimeter, some truly interested, some morbidly curious, but none wanted to plumb the depth of the pain, the guilt, and the loss. And none could. There were only those who had played and those who had watched. And those who had played shunned each other with a vengeance. The glare was too bright, the reflection too painful. So we all pretended we were fans and all the players faded away.

CHAPTER 1

Among the fishing fleet I am known as Captain Hook—crazy Mike Randel the Vietnam vet—and everyone has their own version of what happened out there on the coast last season. Some say I tried to kill my wife—my ex-wife—and to save herself she had to jump overboard. This may be true, if only in an allegorical sense, but I deny homicidal intent. It is also said that I was halfway across the Pacific, headed for Hawaii or Vietnam, when the Coast Guard caught up with me, and that they found me a babbling idiot covered in blood. But I deny ever having been an idiot, babbling or not. It is true that I was locked away in the loony bin, but again I deny having had electroshock or a lobotomy. They did, however, give me a lifetime supply of little blue pills. And they did work. I turned into one mellow dude; life was water off a duck's back as long as I took my pills.

Regardless of the truth of these rumors, I had a reputation as being one bad dude, dangerous and deranged. Unfortunate, because at that moment—just out of the hospital—I was as close to "normal" as I had been since going to Vietnam. I had come to grips (no pun intended for I only had one hand, but perhaps that is why my grip turned out to be so tenuous) with Vietnam, my involvement in it, and my loss of limb. Sad, regrettable, and unchangeable, Vietnam was an intimate part of my personal history. Admittedly, I still felt guilty for my actions and angry over the loss of my arm, but I could live with that.

I went back to my life, living for a time with my folks before finding a place of my own. I considered moving on, but I was a fisherman, and Everett, Washington, was home port. If I was one of its least-favorite sons, then so be it. The good people of Everett—and there were many—would have to accept me. They had raised me to go to war, and I'd be damned if now I'd slither off into some dark hole just to relieve them of the pain of having to look at me.

Freshly schooled in the ways of verbalization, I began, for the first time, to talk to people about Vietnam. I started with my parents, and right off I should have seen that just because I'd found my tongue didn't mean the rest of the world had found their ears. My mother burst into tears and ran from the room even before I got to the good part; and this was no squeamish woman. She'd been a cook on an Alaskan salmon boat for thirty years, had heard it all, but an hour with me was all she could stomach. My father, who'd been a radio operator in the Big One, sat stoically through the morbid details without flinching, said good-night, and went up to bed without another word.

I sat up late, after they abandoned me, smoking cigarettes and trying not to drink. In the wee hours I stole upstairs to the bedroom of my childhood. There, hanging in the closet, palpably close to the glove and its lubricant, were my shroud-covered dress greens. From the breast of the uniform I took my combat infantry badge (a long, thin silver musket on a blue background surrounded by silver oak leaves) and pinned it to my shirt. I wore it always from that night on.

For a time I attended church with my folks, even bought a sports coat to pin my badge to. I had my hair cut, not short but well above my shoulders (I still parted it down the middle and combed it back), and was clean-shaven. I'd lost a good bit of weight in the hospital, mainly from being off the booze, and the puffiness had gone from my face. Looking in the mirror it was impossible to say that I was still young, but at least for a while I was tidy.

At church I tried to make contact with those I recognized (some I knew had lost sons in Vietnam), but uniformly they avoided me. They had heard I was crazy, that I had tried to kill my wife. They saw the hook and the combat insignia, and they quivered for their daughters. In their heart of hearts they rejoiced that their boys had not returned to be like me. The pastor listened patiently, called me son many times, then turned away and washed his hands. Both of them.

My reputation along the waterfront had gone from merely deadly and deranged to deadly, deranged, and obsessed. To my face it was benign tolerance, but behind my back I was the butt of vicious humor. I could find no converts among the fishing fleet, or elsewhere for that matter. Those few vets I ferreted out were uncomfortable, did not want to be seen in my company. I understood. Not long before I would not have welcomed such a person as myself, might even have sunk the hook into them.

To my parents' great relief I soon stopped attending church. I was not angry or depressed. I did not stop shaving or bathing and molt back into a barbarian, but neither did I stop talking about Vietnam with a fervor akin to a holy mission. I spoke of it to all who would listen, and many more who would not.

It wasn't long before my folks asked if I wouldn't be more comfortable in my own place. After all, Leigh Anne—my ex— had moved to Key West and filed for divorce. My folks were never very subtle, but they were right when they said she was not about to rejoin me.

I went on like that through the winter and into the spring. I stayed sober, kept taking my little blue pills, kept going to the brain laundry to see my shrink: a guy named Lance Soblowski, who didn't seem to think I was crazy at all (which made me wonder what his problem was). Mostly we talked about boats and fishing. When it came time to go down to the *Leigh Anne* and start getting her in order for fishing season, he helped me prepare myself for that.

It was early morning, gray, not yet raining. I stood on the dock for a time, just looking, remembering, afraid to board. I hadn't even seen *Leigh Anne,* much less set foot on her, since the Coast Guard had pulled me off more than six months before. She'd been brought around from Westport—out on the coast—by Alan Franklin, one of my few remaining friends from the old days.

For a fishing boat she was unusually smart. (Part of that was Leigh Anne's doing, but my folks had always had smart-looking boats, and I'd learned from them.) She was a double-ender—meaning her stern was pinched in much the same way as her bow—twenty-eight feet in length, all wood and well kept. Her topsides were painted green, trimmed in pale yellow with a gray hull. The wheelhouse was a beauty, much like those found on old tugs: tall and narrow, with an elegantly rounded front and windows set in beneath the lip of a flat roof. A door slid open onto the rear, or aft deck. Here the stack from the engine stood up beside the aft wall of the wheelhouse and rose above it to where the mast held the radar and radio antennae and the crosstree supported the trolling poles.

The actual work of fishing was carried out on the aft deck. Despite being half the length of the boat, and well laid out, the work area was congested, lacking the comfort of the bigger boats. To get from the thigh-deep trolling pit, at the very stern, to the neck-deep fishhold, just short of the wheelhouse, was to run an obstacle course. In between was the trolling cage—an open structure of two-inch pipe uprights and cross-members—which supported the skiff overhead (although not over my head unless I ducked), the skiff's small outboard motor, a bank of power gurdies on each side, and the blocks through which the lines ran. It was an enduring challenge to maneuver the length of the deck, especially for a one-armed man when the deck was slick with fish guts and the boat was pitching in a dirty sea. But such was fishing.

Forward, the wheelhouse stepped down two thirds of its height to a long, flat-roofed cabin that extended almost to the bow, leaving just enough room for the anchor winch and chain locker. This low cabin—with only a foot's width between it and the gunnel—was the roof of the fo'c'sle and galley.

Stepping aboard I was relieved to see that all trace of violence had been cleansed, washed away. No blood splatters trailed across the deck, and when I slid open the door to the wheelhouse I found no telltale traces there either. The cold, lifeless electronics stared back at me: radar for seeing at night and in foul weather; depth-finder for finding bottom; Loran for pinpointing an exact position; compass for plotting a course; CB and VHF radios for communicating.

Maybe they could tell the story of what happened out on the coast between Leigh Anne and me. If only I could link them up and tap their collective memory, surely they would know the truth. Or a better version than the one I'd been left with.

Someone had gone to considerable trouble to straighten out the wheelhouse. Still, it was organized clutter: charts, paperback novels, tools, old coffee cans full of odds and ends of hardware, temporarily empty ashtrays, half a case of empty beer bottles, spit and baling wire. All the trappings of fishing: backbreaking work and boredom.

An unopened pack of cigarettes lay on the chart table. I held the pack, and with the tines of my hook delicately pinched the end of the drawstring and unwound it, removed the rectangle of cellophane, and gently worked open the triangular folds of silver paper. Banging the pack on the hook as if a knuckle, I tapped out a cigarette and putting it to my mouth set fire to it.

On the shelf beneath the wheel I spotted my nonkinetic fish hook. I reached down and brought it out. One of the guys at my father's shop had forged it for me to fish with (my mechanical hook was too dainty to pull and play fish, and all the attendant line and weights involved). The fish hook was just a hunk of steel bent to a question mark and notched like the claw on a tack hammer; it was embedded in a block of wood and wrapped in leather, with a series of belts that strapped to my upper arm and shoulder. I could run stainless fishline through it and with a twist stop it, hold it, and then, with my real hand (no pun intended), pull it in. And it was pointed enough to gaff fish with. Quite the versatile tool. The last time I'd worn it I tried to gaff my wife with it.

I went down the companionway one slow step at a time, ducking my head as I did. I stood at the bottom step, letting the dim shapes of the galley—Leigh Anne had called it the doll-house dinette—come into view: the small alcohol-fueled stove to starboard, to port a narrow table with knee-to-knee benches, and wedged in the bow the double berth. It smelled worse than a fish boat. It smelled of love and hate, sex and rage, tender-ness and terror. Ghosts chortled from every nook and cranny. I fled back up the companionway.

Leigh Anne and I had met in New Mexico four years past. I'd gone to the Southwest because it was so little like the Northwest and Vietnam, both of which were lush and wet. It was dry, unencumbering, and had a decided lack of green. I felt easy there, for a while anyway, although the vast horizons of the desert reminded me of the sea and sometimes left me disoriented, as if the oceans had evaporated around my ankles in the blink of an eye.

I had spent time in the VA Hospital in Seattle after losing my arm in Nam (my hand, actually, and half the forearm—I still had two elbows), hung around Everett for a few years, and went fishing with my folks during the summer as I had most of my life. They owned a Southeast Alaska salmon seiner, but there were too many folks on too small a boat, and I had to get off. Broke Pop's heart, maybe even worse than my losing my arm. I think that's when it hit him: the damage so deep that not even fishing would mend it.

For a number of years I roamed: Canada, Alaska, Mexico. There wasn't much I could do in the way of work with one arm, but then I wasn't much interested. I lived off my disability checks, which just about covered gas and groceries, eventually arriving in the Southwest. I spent time in the desert, around Santa Fe and Albuquerque. I didn't wander through the dry landscape like a prophet or a madman, although there were mo-ments when I felt quite mad, but I did roam, lived out of my truck, ingested drugs, beheld visions, did odd jobs, and met Leigh Anne.

A saloon in Santa Fe named The Rio held my attention for a time. It was somewhat like the intergalactic bar in *Star Wars,* full of oddballs and outlaws of dubious authenticity. When the situation warranted it I'd wear a black patch over one eye to complement the hook and my long hair. (Six feet two, 185, long hair, jeans, cowboy boots, flannel shirt and vest: I knew how to play the role.) Leigh Anne was serving drinks at the time, and had never seen me without the eye patch. I knew she'd been hanging out with some guy, but I also saw that she was interested. One night I tipped her a ten, and when she looked at me in surprise I flipped up the patch and winked at her.

She was a wild girl with an irrepressible spirit, long legs, blond hair, dark eyes, and a goofy smile with dimples that caved in her cheeks. I was mad for her. Too mad for her.

We were married in Reno on the way to Washington. It took less than an hour from the time she popped the question until we were pronounced. We found a couple of plastic rings. Hers was gold with a big red ruby in the shape of a heart. Mine had a little propeller that I worried might fly off and sever one of my fingers. Leigh Anne bought a veil to wear with her halter top and short shorts. I bought a clip-on tie for my T-shirt. She placed her hand gently on top of the hook and said, "I do." When the justice of the peace pronounced us, she blurted out, "The stump! Finally, I get the stump!"

We decided to buy a fishing boat—a troller—and troll for salmon. I'd saved my shares from all those summers fishing with my folks, so we had the money for a boat, but during those early years—or should I say year?—we had each other and little else mattered. We couldn't fuck and fight enough. We were going to fish summers and winter in Hawaii. It was every fisherman's dream.

We even got our dream started. No reason it couldn't have kept on either. I felt good that year, was seldom depressed— the truly black moods had yet to descend. I was drinking, but I could take it or leave it. Of course being in love helped, helped everything: my sex life, my spirit, my purpose.

CHAPTER 2

Looking up from my thoughts, I found an Asian man standing on the dock inspecting *Leigh Anne* as if he were a prospective buyer. He was not of C dock, for there were no Asians on C dock. It took a pass card to get through the gate, and I wondered how he had gotten in, but then the gate didn't always shut properly and that morning I hadn't needed my card. He was oddly dressed in an iridescent-red hat—a Peter Pan–style beanie, with a narrow brim rolled up in back, down in front—plaid wool jacket and shirt—predominantly green and orange—gray polyester trousers, and black street shoes. He looked as if he were on his way to a costume party dressed up as an American.

His jacket collar was up against the rain and his hands were deep in his pockets. Looking at him I thought he might actually be Vietnamese, despite his being too tall and too wide in the shoulders. His face was also a little too broad. So I changed

19

my guess to either Chinese, Korean, or Thai. He backed away and started to move down the dock.

I slid open the wheelhouse door and called after him. "Hey! You want something?"

He stopped and looked back at me, but said nothing. Slowly he retraced half his steps. "I am inquiring of boat to go fishing. Please."

"You want to rent a boat? You know, get a boat for the day, to go fishing?"

He shook his head. "No. I look for job. A job fishing. Deck-hand."

It wasn't raining hard, just a steady Northwest mist, but he seemed indifferent to it. My head was getting wet, poked out the door like it was, so I waved him aboard and pulled myself back in.

He moved cautiously down the finger of cement that separated my boat from the next. When he came amidships he hesitated, and I had to go to the door and again tell him to come aboard.

He stepped up onto the gunnel and down onto the deck, but he was reluctant to enter the wheelhouse.

"Come on in outta the rain. Come on. I don't bite."

He came to the door and peered in, took the measure of the small room, and decided against it. With a half-smile he backed away and stood staring at me.

I moved to the doorway, fished out my smokes, and, tapping the pack against the hook, offered him one. He nodded, stepped cautiously up to take it, all the while his eyes moved rapidly from the hook to my combat infantry badge to the cigarette to my eyes and around again. A Zippo burned suddenly at the end of my cigarette.

I nodded. "You are Chinese?"

"Vietnamese," he insisted.

"Boat person?"

"Yes. I may sit here?" he asked, indicating the hatch cover to the fishhold.

I raised my cigarette in the affirmative. He stepped up onto the shin-high hatch cover and squatted!

I cringed.

The squat heaped scorn on a civilization that for decades had strived to perfect the La-Z-Boy recliner. It was at once positive and monolithic, ancient, resigned, and defiant. The simple motion of lowering the pelvis to the heels repudiated everything that Americans had been told they were fighting for in Vietnam. How could you bring democracy to a country where every member of the citizenry, regardless of age, rank, sex, or social status, could squat in equality?

"You have been here, in America, how long?"

He smoked the cigarette with great deliberation, and no little satisfaction I thought. He turned over his wrist to inspect the face of his digital watch. "Fourteen month, five day."

"And you want to be a fisherman?"

He nodded.

"Well, you're a might early. Fishing doesn't start for a couple three months." I thought I noticed a faintly ironic smile at the corner of his mouth.

"Last year I told I too late."

"Who told you that?"

"Everyone."

I nodded. "You live here, in Everett?"

"Seattle."

"What are you doing up here?"

"I look all places with fishing boat."

"You been to Gig Harbor?"

He nodded. "Tacoma, Bremerton. All over. No one want Vietnamese deckhand." He eyed the hook.

What did he think? Did the hook mean I'd for sure need help? Did he associate it with my combat badge, or with Vietnam? We were certainly both refugees from the same place, the same war.

It wasn't easy to get on a boat these days, not even for a white American. The Northwest economy was so fucked up that every logger and laid-off mill hand was looking for a fishing job. But the bottom line, of course, was that he was Vietnamese.

There'd already been big trouble in the Gulf with the Vietnamese trying to break into the shrimping fleet. In the Northwest the white fishermen were enraged that the Supreme Court had upheld Judge Boldt's interpretation of an old treaty that gave the local Indians half the salmon catch in Puget Sound. So any other group of "foreigners" trying to get a toehold was met with great hostility.

I looked at him closely. He could as easily have been sixty as forty. His face was creased, eyes weary but ever so alert. A gook for a deckhand. I almost laughed out loud. That would cement my reputation.

"Mike Randel," I said suddenly, almost leaping out of the wheelhouse, my left hand extended.

He came up quickly, eyes on the hook. Taking one step aft he weighted his back leg. For a split second I thought he might put me on my ass, knew he could do it, realized my foolishness at having moved so suddenly, and caught myself up short.

The apparent danger passed and he put out his right hand. I quickly grasped it with my left, as I could see he was confused as to how you shook the hand of a man with a hook.

"Tu Van Huyen. I most pleased to meet you, Cap'n Ran'l."

"Randel, with a dee."

"Yes. Ran'l."

"Call me Mike."

He nodded. I offered him another cigarette. He refused and I again took up my position in the doorway. "You sure you don't want to come in out of the rain?"

"Yes, I oh-kay. Thank you." Again he squatted.

"You speak good English."

He shrugged. "I study."

"You just pick it up since coming to the States?"

"No. I in Malaysia for one year five month in refugee camp. English lady give English lessons. I study very much."

"A year and a half? No shit. From Vietnam to Malaysia, by boat?"

He nodded. "Two month on boat. Very small boat . . ." He glanced quickly about *Leigh Anne*. "Apology. Very much bigger this boat, but many, many people."

"Two months." I whistled. "Long time. At least you've got some experience being on a small boat in close quarters." Was that why he declined to enter the wheelhouse? "Same as fishing." I laughed.

He looked down and beneath the short brim of his Day-Glo hat I could see his forehead crease. "Not to argue, Cap'n Ran'l, but not same as fishing. Many people starve. Myself, I lose eight kilo. Two times we robbed by pirates. All things of value stole from us. The women are raped. I protest and am beaten." He looked up at me briefly to make certain the point was made, which it was.

"What'd you do in Vietnam?"

"Soldier," he said flatly.

ARVN. Shit. Every American soldier in Vietnam had hated the Army of the Republic of Vietnam. They'd been a lazy bunch of undisciplined cowards. I immediately felt a degree of contempt for the man. Still, I tempered it as best I could with the thought that he had probably been a brave man, and that we had fought a common enemy and lost.

Again I offered him a cigarette and this time he accepted. Before he could pull out his Zippo I opened a small box of wooden matches and, using the hook, extracted one, lit it, and held it out. He examined the hook closely as I set fire to his cigarette.

"This . . ." He pointed at my prosthesis.

"Hook."

"Hook?"

I nodded.

"How do you come by it?"

"Vietnam."

He didn't look up but continued to examine the mechanical device protruding from the sleeve of my jacket. He raised his cigarette to his face, covering his mouth and chin as he did, and inhaled deeply. "And this?" he asked, smoke spilling from his lips. He patted his chest lightly and pointed to the badge on my jacket. "Vietnam also?"

I nodded. His face betrayed nothing. Did he reflect on the times he had narrowly missed losing a leg or an arm? Did he hold me in esteem for having fought for his country? I didn't, because I'd never fought for his country. I'd fought because my father and my country told me to. I didn't give a shit about Vietnam or the Vietnamese, but neither had my father nor my country.

He cleared his throat. "The war for independence of Vietnam very costly to many people. I am certain you were most brave." He stood and stepped to the rail and field-stripped his cigarette. Shaking the tobacco into the water, he rolled the paper into a tiny ball that disappeared into his pocket.

Old habits die hard, I thought.

"Better I look someplace other to fish," he said, then swung a leg over the rail and stepped down onto the float.

"Wait." When he did I didn't know what to say. We stood staring at each other.

It was a curse, the guilt I felt for the Vietnamese (all Orientals are Vietnamese to me, even preppie Japanese-American college math majors). I could not escape from it. Squalor evoked Vietnam guilt. Even back alleys could trigger it if just the right combination of discarded artifacts and odor—usually twisted metal and decaying vegetation—were properly aligned. Panhandlers were all Vietnamese. Whenever they approached me on the street I never let them off with less than a quarter. But I had to imagine these beggars to be Vietnamese, because they never were. Orientals never begged, never looked you in the eye when they passed on the street, never allowed you the opportunity to assuage your guilt.

"Look, I'm going to need someone." I shrugged. "Is there somewhere I can get ahold of you, when the time comes?"

He looked at me with his flat face and eyes barely uncovered, but did not speak.

"What's the matter, GI number ten?" I laughed awkwardly. "We were both soldiers. We both lost the war. Maybe we can help each other out."

"The Red Dragon," he said finally. "In Chinatown. You call there, leave message." He turned and walked away in a rain he seemed not to notice. I saw that he had a slight limp, but he walked tall down the row of boats, through the gate, up the ramp, and out of sight.

CHAPTER 3

Leigh Anne took up my days, and I was content to putter away. It was therapeutic, an advanced form of occupational therapy. I was still taking those little blue pills, but I had begun to break them in half along the conveniently provided crease. I felt at ease, or a good deal closer to it than I had in a long while.

I replaced the double berth in the bow of the fo'c'sle with narrow bunks to starboard. To port I put up a coatrack and above it a couple of small lockers. I covered everything with a fresh coat of gray paint. It wasn't absolutely necessary, but it kept me busy. Once a week I had supper with my folks. I made no more confessions, they didn't mention Leigh Anne (the divorce papers had come through), and generally everything between us was, on the surface, just rosy.

I think I had become an embarrassment to them, and that hurt me deeply. Everett, despite its boom, was still a small town at heart. And the fishing community bordered on incestuous, so interwoven were the relationships. My family was known

25

and knew; knew what the community thought of their son: the crazed Vietnam vet with the hook. Ever since the "incident" and my release from the hospital and my conversion—you could call me a born-again Vietnam vet—I'd become an even bigger source of embarrassment to them.

The Riptide had been my hangout since before I was old enough to drink. It was a local tavern—beer and wine, a couple of pool tables—not far off the main drag, close to the waterfront. The first time I had ventured in was with my pal Duncan. We had both just graduated from high school. I was going off to the United States Army, and he was headed back East to some Ivy League college. It was to be our final summer of common experience.

At midday the tavern had been empty except for the bartender and the pinochle game in back. The bartender was drying glasses and took his time stepping over. Hands flat on the bar, he looked us in the eye and said, "What'll it be, *boys*?"

"Make it a couple of drafts," I replied, slow and casual. But my voice cracked, and the bartender broke into laughter.

Out on the sidewalk Duncan said, "That was good. You really handled that well. Now, how 'bout an ice cream cone?"

A year and a half and a lifetime of experience later, still not twenty-one: Duncan's hair fell to his shoulders, and he had grown something on his top lip that he referred to as his moustaches. Me, I was sporting an eye patch and, in place of my right hand, a hook. It was a Friday evening and the place was crowded. We wedged ourselves in at the bar.

"What'll you boys have?" It was the same bartender.

Before he, or I, knew what had happened I had him by the shirt with the hook. I lifted the eye patch to look at him squarely. Informed him that he was speaking to a combat veteran of the Vietnam War, and that I'd ceased being a *boy* some time back.

Those at the bar stopped their drinking. The bartender whined something inaudible and I released him.

"Two drafts," I snarled, lowering the eye patch.

"Subtle," Duncan said. "Very subtle. You learn that in *The Nam*?"

He was the only shithead intellectual draft-dodging antiwar protester I'd have taken that from. In fact, he was the only one I'd get near. He was home for Christmas, and we spent ten days continuously blitzed on a vast array of drugs, rapping about Vietnam. Strangely enough it was me that did most of the talking. And not in general political terms, which I had no use for, but the nuts and bolts of daily living for a grunt and a helicopter-door gunner.

Even in the hospital, endlessly hanging out with other vets, I hadn't talked about it so much. But Vietnam was on the tip of Duncan's tongue; the invasion of Cambodia and the Kent State shootings were not long past. He was feeling part of an army that had finally entered combat and begun taking casualties. He seemed truly threatened, and maybe it was his arrogance in thinking that what he was involved in was any more than an unauthorized sort of NCAA sport that got me talking.

Days later, after interminable hours of speed raps, having said everything we had to say a dozen times in a dozen different ways, I understood that the peace movement was not out to get me. At least when I finally came down I remembered that that was what I'd understood.

Duncan disappeared after that. Some stories have it that he went underground, while others have him smuggling drugs in the Caribbean. Whatever happened, I credit that Christmas week with having helped me keep my sanity as long as I did.

For years afterward the corner stool in the Riptide was reserved for me, and no one with any sense sat on it when I was around. The next one over was Duncan's, and nobody sat on it either, unless they were invited, 'cause I expected Duncan to be joinin' me anytime.

So when I got out of the hospital (for my head, not my hand), the folks at the Riptide were somewhat startled when I didn't take up my old stool but sat at the middle of the bar and ordered soda water. Folks shied away from me more than ever. No longer drunk and disorderly, I really got the cold shoulder. I don't know if it was the incident out on the coast and my internment in the booby hatch, or just the new me, with my combat badge and a cause.

Whatever, people didn't know how to deal with me, and given a choice preferred not to. The stool beside me was no longer reserved for Duncan, but whoever sat in it had to listen to my rap, and it remained no less empty than when I had shown fangs and drooled blood. Stumping for the Vietnam vet won me few friends, and in the end I kept my own counsel, no longer went to the Riptide, stopped going to church, and seldom saw my folks. I worked on *Leigh Anne* or stayed home, and what the Riptide had been unable to do, my isolation finally did: I began to drink again.

4

CHAPTER

As the opening of fishing season drew near, I became obsessed with Tu Van Huyen. It was as if he and I were the only two Vietnam vets in the world. If we could find no support from the country that put us to war, then I determined we would support each other. One night I took myself to Seattle and the Red Dragon.

It was just the sort of neo-Oriental place I imagined: dim red lighting, black walls and ceiling, red trim, pagoda roof above the bar, and red dragons on the wall. It was longer than it was wide, with tables in back and a smooth black-lacquer bar top. Behind the bar stood an Oriental woman wearing a "Suzie Wong" dress. She looked to be in her fifties and was a hard but attractive woman. She walked to the end of the bar where I had taken a stool near the door, laid her red fingernails on the black lacquer, and asked what I wanted.

The tip of her nose and her tiny mouth seemed unto their own, disembodied from her eyes, which floated high above on her round, broad face. Despite this there was something sensuous about her.

"I'll have a Seven-and-Seven and Tu Van Huyen."

She glanced at the hook then turned away to fix my drink.

I was in the heart of enemy territory. Excluding the black man sitting at the other end of the bar, I was the only non-Oriental in the place. In back were two older guys and a couple of sharply dressed young women I thought might be pros. The other half dozen customers were men sitting alone or in pairs.

"What is it you wish to speak to Mr. Van Huyen about?" the bartender asked, setting my drink before me.

"Well," I said, taking a sip, "it's kind of personal." I smiled, but her expression remained unchanged. "He told me I'd find him here."

"He may be in later."

"I'll wait."

"As you wish."

I waited, smoked, drank more whiskey. Looking about the dimly lit room, with its small red orbs burning on the tables, Asian faces, and pretty flirtatious girls giggling in back, I was unavoidably reminded of R and R. For five days me and a bro' from my unit had drunk and screwed our way around Hong Kong in dozens of places like the Red Dragon. It had been the last time I had had two hands with which to make love to a woman.

Love by the hour or the week with sweet young Chinese girls. They had been wonderful, although I could never get it out of my head that they were peasants in disguise, that really they belonged in the paddies with their black pants rolled above their knees, backs bent to cultivation. I also couldn't help but feel that I was exploiting them, the warrior American fucking the peasant girls, but they didn't seem to mind as they folded my money into their purses, exploiting my loneliness, leaving me limp and a long ways from home.

When I looked up from my drink and saw her walking across the room, I thought she was coming for me. She was stunning. Tiny. Black glossy hair cut blunt to her shoulders. Small delicate features, red lips. She wore a short white jacket over a green-striped silk dress that barely covered her knees. She had fantastic legs and toy feet wedged into incredibly high heels.

Without once glancing my way she walked up behind me to the cigarette machine. When I heard the coins fall I turned to see her bent at the waist, practically on tiptoe in her heels, slit in her dress showing thigh, the curve of her ass irresistible.

The silk of her dress felt like a bit of heaven beneath my hand. And the firm curve of her cheek was paradise. But, as always, paradise was short-lived. Seconds later her escort was at her side and both of them were giving me holy hell.

I had startled myself as much as her, never having accosted a woman in public before. I tried to apologize, but it didn't get me far. She hurled insults at me as if I were a dart board. Her boyfriend—neat in his three-piece suit and slight paunch—was closing fast like he needed to make a good impression.

My lingering Oriental guilt was temporarily displaced by my need to survive. Wasn't that what happened when you went to war? The brain-of-the-dog grinned from jowl to jowl, sanity was supplanted by survival. You might spend your life trying to make amends, but suddenly you were right back in the same old situation with the same old response: Get 'em before they get you.

Too late he saw the hook as I grabbed him up under the balls. I edged a half-step closer so that we were chest up to each other, with me looking down into his face. In the red light I could see the perspiration beading up on his high forehead.

"Tell her to shut up," I said, tugging gently at his crotch to emphasize my meaning. He said something to her and she quieted. "Now, convey to the lady my deepest apologies. It was very rude of me, and I had no call to treat her that way." He translated my words, although I felt he lacked a certain sincerity in his delivery. The woman seemed unconvinced as she stood stone-faced boring holes into the side of my head.

By now the other couple was almost on top of us, and I could see that the second fellow was thinking to free his friend. Suddenly an arm came up around his neck and the face of Tu Van Huyen appeared from over his shoulder.

"Cap'n Ran'l. Please, what is trouble?" he demanded.

"I don't know." I looked into the face of the man I had by the balls. "Anything wrong?" He shook his head no. "You accept my apology?" He nodded yes. "And the lady?" Again he nodded. "Good." I loosened my grip and took a step back. Tu let go of the other fellow and both couples turned and fled.

Immediately the bartender lit into Tu, barraging him in French. Tu tried to defend himself—certainly he couldn't have been defending me—but to no avail. Her angry words chased us both out into the night.

Tu was highly agitated. He headed up the street and I went with him, then abruptly he did an about-face, leaving me in my tracks, then did another before I could catch up with him and headed back in my direction.

"You have caused me great embarrassment," he said suddenly, slowing to a halt. "This woman very good to me. She give me job, room to live in. Why you do this?" He pointed at my hook and shook his head, started to pace again.

"Look," I said as he came by again. "It wasn't your fault, it was mine. I'll go in and tell her I'm sorry."

"Sorry? What is sorry?" He stopped again. "You sorry to this woman you touch. What is that?"

"I *am* sorry. You have no idea. It was just . . ." I threw up my arms. "Just a mistake."

"Very big mistake. Maybe I have no more job at Red Dragon. No job, no room. What then?"

"Come fishing with me."

"With you?"

"Yeah."

"I think not."

"Why?"

"Not so good idea I think." He shook his head.

"But . . ." I was suddenly panicked that he might actually refuse. "Tu, you've got to go fishing with me."

"Why?"

"Well . . . because you'd make a good deckhand."

"Many fishermen in Everett. You not need Tu."

"Yes, I do. You and I are just alike . . ."

He shook his head.

"Yes, we are. We're both refugees from Vietnam. Nobody gives a shit about us. Nobody will fish with me because they think I'm *dinky-dau*. Nobody will take you fishing because you're a gook.''

"No! Do not say this. Never! I am Vietnamese.''

"No, you're not, you're Chinese; that's why they threw you out of Vietnam.''

"No! It was mistake. I am Vietnamese.''

I don't know how I saw it, or how I managed to get myself and Tu to the sidewalk in time, but when the gun went off we were already on our way down. I suppose it might not have been them—the woman I had insulted and her friends—after all, I had apologized. It might just have been random street violence, but it's doubtful. It was a Mercedes, and the color—white—may have been what first caught my eye. I couldn't see the passengers, other than as dark objects, but I did see something protrude from the passenger window as the car raced up to us. I could see it, black against the white of the door, and the brain-of-the-dog barked, "Gun." I threw a blind-side tackle on Tu just before it sounded.

Ambushed! I couldn't believe it. Tu and I got up running. We slipped into the alley halfway up the block. For a moment, with the light cut by the canyon walls of the buildings and the sound of gunfire still echoing in my ears, I thought I was on patrol and wished for an M-60, a brace of claymores, and the Mercedes to approach once more.

Lights suddenly erupted into the alley. Tu and I pressed ourselves into a doorway. The engine roared and the lights sped toward us. Brake lights flashed red as the squad car intersected with the street and turned right toward the Red Dragon. Tu and I ran down the alley in the direction from which the cops had come.

When we reached the next block I started to go north, but a whistle from Tu brought me back, and I followed him up a stairway behind the Red Dragon. We went up to the second floor and down a dark hallway into a room lit only by the lights of the street. A sweeping red light roamed the walls. We stood in the corners, by the edge of the window, and looked down at the scene on the street.

The squad car was double-parked, its bank of lights flashing.

One of Seattle's finest stood with a foot in the open door and spoke into his radio. Across the street an elderly Oriental couple had stopped, but otherwise the night was quiet.

Tu motioned me back from the window and indicated I take the bed. I guessed we were in his room: a sparsely furnished little place with bare walls, a single bed, a table, one chair, and a hot plate.

"What if she tells 'em we're up here?"

"Not to worry."

"What makes you so sure? She was plenty pissed."

"I know."

I let it drop. It didn't matter much one way or the other. We hadn't done anything, unless it was a crime to be shot at. The way I figured it, the less I had to do with the police the better. I didn't know if Tu was legal, but I doubted he wanted any run-ins with the law either way.

Shortly we heard the car doors slam and the red light ceased to stroke the walls.

Tu went to the window and looked out. "What is it they would do with us if we are catch?"

"Caught. If we are caught. Nothin'. We ain't done nothin'. They'd ask us a bunch of questions. Separate us. Question us one at a time."

"Yes, this is good tactic. What then?"

"That's it."

"We run."

"They were shooting at us."

After a moment he said, "For long time I have not been shooted at."

"Shot at."

There was a light tap at the door. I started to get up, but Tu motioned me to stay. He opened the door and the bartender from the Red Dragon slipped in. She turned her back to me and held a hushed conversation with Tu then let herself out.

"Well?"

"She says to them nothing. But I must go. These men you" —he cupped his crotch— "she has seen before. She afraid they come back, make trouble for me, for her."

"Good. Let's go."

"Where?"

"Everett. Can you leave your stuff here?"

He nodded. "What will I do? Where will I sleep? What will I eat?"

"Do you want to go fishing or not?"

"Yes, very much. But with you? I not know."

"You can sleep on the boat, help me get it ready for the season. I'll feed you and take it out of your share when we start fishing."

Tu was silent. The light from the street cast a dim glow on his down-turned face.

"Doesn't look to me like you've got much choice."

"Yes," he said solemnly. "I think I am becoming boat person again without my choosing."

"You're right. Can you drive me back here?"

He looked at his watch. "What will I do? Where will I sleep? What will I eat?"

"Do you want to go hungry or not?"

"Yes, very much, but with what? I am happy."

"You're a beggar, he said. I can get it, the hard way, the hard season. I'll feed you and take care of you then when we go fishing."

"It was silent." One drink from this safe cost a dollar to a car. Is he a drunkard?

"Doesn't he go to the brewery to get drunk then?"

"Yes," he said softly. "And I am sure this is not so bad without any drinking."

CHAPTER 5

Tu settled in aboard *Leigh Anne,* and while he didn't complain, he was clearly not happy. Instead of making him feel like he was in my debt by running a tab, I put him on an hourly wage and let him buy his own food. When I went home at night the boat was his, so I really didn't see what he had to complain about. Soon we'd be fishing and a halfway decent season would put some money in his pocket. If it worked out between us, he might become a steady partner; and while the chances of his ever making enough as a deckhand to buy his own boat and license were slim, this was, as I reminded him, America, and anything was possible.

Yes, he told me, so he'd read.

With the weather starting to warm and the opening of salmon season not long off, we moved *Leigh Anne* around to the ship-yard and had her hauled. And there—up on a cradle looking as improbable as a whale in an aquarium—I discovered a cracked plank. I had no recollection of having hit anything, but it certainly explained the noticeable increase in water that stood in the bilge.

The plank in question was well up from the garboard, but nonetheless below the waterline. It posed no immediate threat, and in all likelihood would have lasted out the season, but that wasn't the way I liked to play the game. I liked to stay even, keep ahead when possible.

What should have been at most a two-day project—bottom paint, replace the zincs, and pack the stuffing box—would now take at least a week. Good boat wood was no longer easy to come by, and I would not get what I needed in Everett. Seattle would be the closest source, but I had a friend in Port Townsend who was a shipwright. He and his wife had recently had a baby, and I'd been meaning to go up for a visit.

I phoned Paddy and he invited me up to stay the night, certain he could lay his hands on what I needed. I took the Mukilteo ferry late that afternoon—leaving Tu in charge of *Leigh Anne*—drove up Whidbey Island to Keystone, and crossed, again by ferry, to Port Townsend. It was to be a night of extremes: pleasure for me, terror for Tu.

Paddy and his wife, Sue, lived in a wonderful house in the woods with their two-month-old daughter, Sarah. Paddy was a tall, lanky fellow who had been the tennis star at our high school and had given up the good life his parents had prepared him for to become a boat builder. Sue was a voluptuous brunette, just as cute and stubborn as could be. Their daughter was beautiful with her mother's round, rosy face. And their house was one that only a shipwright would build, with hardly a right angle in the place.

As a pair of tall, good-looking high school jocks, Paddy and I had been lumped together—despite the differences in our backgrounds—and had been fairly good friends. But he had gone on to the University of Washington and our paths diverged.

After the war I bumped into him in Everett. I was wearing the hook and the eye patch, while he had on a top hat, tuxedo T-shirt, and hair down to his shoulders. He was startled to see me. Then I flipped up the eye patch with a wink, and we had a good laugh. Though we seldom saw each other, we remained friends.

They were a disgustingly happy family. Sue made me feel welcome, cooked a great meal, and the three of us stayed up late playing with the baby and talking. They never asked any embarrassing questions about Leigh Anne or the hospital. In the morning Paddy took me down to the co-op boat works to which he belonged and pulled out a beautiful piece of Port Orchard cedar. He refused to take my money, although I knew that as a boat builder he was barely scraping by. So after much haranguing I accepted, but only on the condition he build himself a salmon smoker, which I assured him he would have need of in the near future.

I said good-bye and caught the early ferry back to Keystone. It was an exquisite spring morning. A crisp nor'easter had come up during the night, blowing every hint of gray from the sky. Crossing from Port Townsend, on what was almost a toy ferry, was a dream. The jagged Cascades lay like the blade of a misery whip against a sky of glacial blue. To the north and south were the heights of Mounts Baker and Rainier, while behind me to the west, the Olympics. Bathed in the brilliance of the morning light, the Olympics rose fir-covered from the water's edge to snowy peaks. And all about me were the cold blue waters of Puget Sound and the Strait of Juan de Fuca.

It was the Northwest at its magnificent best. Not a rare day, but one that was nonetheless all too infrequent. Between these times it was not hard to forget that such days existed, leaving you to wonder just why anyone in his right mind would voluntarily live in a world that was gray, cold, and rain-soaked more often than not. And then remarkably such a day as this would suddenly appear and you remembered why indeed you did live here, and you knew there was no place else you'd rather be.

Disembarking from the ferry, I felt infused with the day and a lingering sense of well-being imparted to me from Paddy and Sue. The Dodge Power Wagon was running smooth. I had a fine piece of wood flagged behind me as I sailed down Whidbey Island, crossed again at Mukilteo, and went straight to the boatyard.

And there my exuberance died. Printed in bold block letters across the faded bottom paint of *Leigh Anne* were the words NO GOOKS.

I stopped the truck and sat with the engine running and the anger rising inside me. Tools, sandpaper, zincs, and cans of paint lay scattered about. Half-burned sticks of wood, black and cold like burned crosses, pointed out the extent of the ugliness. Up in the cradle *Leigh Anne* looked vulnerable; caught with her pants down they had branded her bottom.

The wheelhouse door slid back, and Tu peered cautiously down at the truck before stepping out onto the deck. I shut off the engine and got out. I took the end of the ladder as Tu lowered it over the side and climbed down without speaking. We stood staring at the hull with its warning.

It must have been a terrifying scene, not unlike the KKK come to call. The words were seared into the hull and would not easily come away. Tu looked truly tired, as if he had finally seen one cruelty too many. He told me he had been up all night, sure that they would set the boat on fire. We gathered the scattered equipment, then stood once more staring silently at the epitaph. The real damage was negligible, but emotionally I felt as if I'd been kicked in the balls. From the despondent look on Tu's face it was obvious that he felt the same way.

"Come on, let's get some breakfast."

I deliberately took us to where we'd be most liable to run into someone who, if not directly involved, would know who was. We went into Vic's and took a booth. At the counter a couple of young fishermen who I knew couldn't read were studying their eggs as if *The New York Times* was printed on them. They weren't the ones, but they weren't as ignorant as they looked. In a booth at the back were four old-time seine skippers, peers of Pop's. They weren't the ones either, but I didn't doubt that they also knew, and probably approved.

The boys at the counter ate up quickly and left. I ordered big, while Tu had only tea and toast. I blamed myself for what had happened and figured Tu was probably plenty pissed at me. I knew there was a lot of resentment toward him. Everyone knew I had a Vietnamese deckhand by then, and no one liked it. But most people figured I was dangerous enough not to confront.

"Cap'n Mike," Tu said, after the waitress had refilled my

coffee and his tea. "I am ashamed for this. You give me to guard the boat and I fail."

"It wasn't your fault," I insisted.

"Yes, yes. I do not know what to do when these men come. They are five. They come suddenly. It is dark. I think they are drunk. They are calling me, and you, all the most bad kind of names. They have fire. For sure I am thinking they are going to burn the boat and me. I want very much do something, but I have no gun, nothing." Tu looked at me from across the table, and I could see the humiliation and rage on his face.

I felt horrible that he had had to endure such abuse. That he held himself responsible was more than I could bear. "Tu, it's not your fault. It's not your job to guard the boat. You're a deckhand, not a sentry. I'm just glad you weren't hurt. And the boat is okay."

He didn't look convinced. He leaned back and stared into his tea. I lit a cigarette and called to the waitress for the check. Just then the old-timers who'd been sitting in the back walked by.

"Morning, Mike," old man Metcalf said.

"Vince." I nodded, looking up at the group.

"Your daddy know you're fishin' with this fella?"

I studied my cigarette for a moment, then looked up at him. "I can't say one way or the other, Vince, but for sure he knows you got shit for brains."

The other skippers chuckled and one of them gently pushed Metcalf down the aisle and out the door.

I paid up, and we went back to work.

6

CHAPTER

I avoid guns. Once you have fired a machine gun—any gun for that matter—in anger, and seen the results, up close, your perspective changes. "Guns don't kill, only people do," or so Friends of the Gun would have you believe; and, in an absolute sense, there is some validity to their argument. But those who have been combatants—slept with weapons, used them more often than their toothbrushes—know the way of guns, their predilection to self-will. So it was not without great hesitancy that I scrounged through the wheelhouse cabinets looking for my semiautomatic .22 caliber rifle.

I kept it for sharks. I had tried to fish without it, but one day I hooked twenty-three salmon heads, and the next day I bought the rifle. Of course, I hadn't had any trouble since. Not until the night before, when I'd again been caught unprepared. But no more.

Tu was intrigued by the way the rifle broke down into its stalk. I only had to tear it apart once and he could put it together blindfolded. He broke it down and reassembled it a couple of times before handing it back to me with a nod of approval. We left it in plain sight, unloaded, and went back to work.

The days were mild and each one was longer than the one preceding. Tu was a hard worker, learned fast, and had good dexterity. We scrubbed, sanded, sawed, painted, and packed. We also had a visitor: Pop Randel.

I hadn't seen him for weeks. And when he hadn't shown up after Tu signed on, I began to think he might not, ever. Somewhat leery of his appearance at this particular time, I was nonetheless glad to see him.

My father had a great sense of propriety. If your country called you went. If you lost a limb you didn't look back. You married, had kids, and stayed married. You went to the lodge on Wednesday, got drunk on Friday, and went to church on Sunday. Life was simple. And you didn't fish with foreigners, unless their names were Kelly, Swirsky, or Spediachi.

He hoisted himself from the cab of his pickup, eyeing the rifle and Tu as he did. We were in the process of fastening down the new plank.

"Howdy, Pop."

"Mike."

The screw set tight, and I came away from the boat leaving Tu to hold the butt end of the plank in place.

"Can we talk?" He jerked his thumb toward the truck, meaning away from Tu.

"Sure. By the way, I'd like you to meet my new deckhand. Tu, this is my father, Carl Randel."

Tu smiled and stretched out his arms, one to hold the plank and the other to shake my father's hand.

"Pop, this is Tu Van Huyen."

Tu's extended hand was three feet short of its mark. Reluctantly my father stepped forward. Actually he only took half a step then leaned as far forward as he could so as not to get too close. He touched Tu's hand briefly, mumbled something, and turned back to his pickup. He had a line of floats coiled in the bed of his truck. I tapped one of them with the hook.

" 'Bout that time again," I said.

He nodded, took the cigarettes from his breast pocket, and lit up. He still kept himself in reasonable trim. His eyes were clear. He didn't drink heavily. He owned his own diesel-repair shop and worked regularly when he wasn't up in Southeast Alaska fishing. It was just that his brain had solidified. The future had become low-tar cigarettes and light beer.

What had happened to my hero? The man who'd plunged into those icy Alaskan waters when I was just a kid and going down fast; the man who had bought me my first can of Gloveolium and had shown me the way to the porcelain altar after my first drunk; the man who had encouraged me to join the army after high school, when I was not yet eighteen, because he'd done the same and it had made a man out of him; the man who had stood tight-lipped and deeply confused when I came home with just one hand. At first I had been his wounded war hero; now I was just an embarrassment.

"Mike, why are you doin' this?" He sounded truly bewildered. "Why don't you get rid of this guy, come fishin' with your mom and me? We won't be able to fish much longer. Then the boat'll be yours."

Finally: the annual bribe. I'd begun to think that maybe he was so pissed off he wouldn't make the offer this year. And actually I felt relieved that things, bad as they were, hadn't gotten beyond guilt and bribery.

I pulled my smokes from my pocket, shook one loose, and plucked it from the packet with the hook. The old man fired his Bic and held it out to me without looking. I didn't move, and after a pause he was forced to turn his head and move the lighter closer to the cigarette and the hook. I peered across the flame into his narrow eyes and saw him squirm.

"Your mother wants you to come to dinner Thursday night," he said angrily, climbing back into the cab and slamming the door.

"Can I bring Tu?"

"No, goddamn it! Seven o'clock and try to be on time for a change." He spun the tires in the gravel and roared off.

Tu, who was usually quiet, was quieter than usual. Hardly a word passed between us that afternoon. Not until our work was done and we were perched up on the deck—we were both sleeping on board—barbecuing chicken on the hibachi, did we begin to speak.

"Tu, is your father still alive?" I asked, leaning back in my beach chair, legs up on the gunnel, beer in hand.

He shook his head. "No, my father long time dead. French kill him when I small boy."

"You got any family?"

Again he shook his head. "All dead." He squatted beside the hibachi on the fishhold cover with a cigarette resting with peculiar sophistication between the tips of two upward-pointing fingers. He spoke matter-of-factly. "At end of World War Two there is famine in Vietnam. Two million peoples die."

"Two million?"

He nodded and drew slowly on his cigarette, letting the smoke drift out through his nose. "All old peoples die. Gran'father, gran'mother, also my mother, one brother, three sister, many cousin. The French and Japanese do nothing. Let people starve."

"Why? Were the French and Japanese in it together?"

It was the first but by no means the last time that Tu regarded me with quiet contempt for my ignorance concerning not only the history of his country but also my own.

"After French surrender to Germany in Europe, they surrender Vietnam to Japan. French very good at surrender."

"How long were the French in Vietnam?"

"One hundred years."

"No shit?"

"No shit." Tu stepped over to the rail and field-stripped his butt. "May I tell something to you, Mike?"

"Hell yes!" I raised my beer. "Free speech is the American way."

Tu opened himself a beer, squatted beside the hibachi, and turned the chicken. "How is it that you would go to war, very far away war, to fight a people about you know nothing? I notice this of American people since I come here. You know nothing of history. American Revolution more important to Vietnamese than people of America I think. How is this so?"

He turned to me as if I might actually have an answer, which, of course, I didn't. But he was right: I had virtually no knowledge of Vietnamese history and precious little more of American. I could only shrug and with a smirk say, "I was only seventeen when I went in the army. What'd I know?"

"I am thirteen," he replied, looking away to hide his contempt.

"Congratulations," I said angrily. "So, the French killed your family?"

"Yes." He stood up abruptly and walked into the wheelhouse and went below. A moment later he was back with paper plates and a pan of beans. He filled a plate with chicken and beans and handed it to me. We ate in silence.

The Olympic Mountains were visible from our perch. Clear and pink-tinged in the setting sun, they looked to be a backdrop for a movie set—cardboard cutouts—so clean were their edges.

"You should not argue with father," Tu suddenly said.

"What?" I almost choked on my beans.

"It is never good to argue with father."

"Can I quote you on that?"

"What does this mean?"

"It means my father is a fucking jerk."

"Still, he is father."

"Tu, my father and I do not see things the same way. He thinks I should do things different than how I do them. He thinks his way is the right way, the only way."

"Perhaps he is right. Sometimes it difficult for the son to understand wisdom of the father."

"I'll tell you what, ol' buddy, I listened to my father once, and this is what it got me." I raised the hook. "If I listened to him again you'd be back in Seattle sweeping out the Red Dragon."

"Perhaps it is best."

"You don't like it here? Then get the hell off my boat. I ain't stoppin' you." With that I got up and went below deck.

CHAPTER 7

Tu stayed. We let the question of my father's wisdom slide. A few days later we put *Leigh Anne* back in the water and motored her around to the slip. It being Thursday, I went off to have dinner with my folks as instructed, leaving Tu with the .22, loaded.

Like many older homes in Everett, my family's was above street level, with the garage around back off the alley. The entire block was that way, with the lawns rising and dropping sharply from the curb on opposite sides of the street. Neatly trimmed hedges and rosebushes framed the small clapboard-and-stucco houses, and an occasional pine or magnolia stood in the front yard.

It was a white working-class neighborhood: Christian, patriotic, entrenched. They paid their taxes, went to church, sent their sons to war. The fathers were tradesmen or small-business men. The women made babies and canned fruit, a few held jobs. Their children played Little League (only the boys in my day), went to school, some even to college (despite the lip service paid education, it wasn't highly regarded), went off to war and never came home or came home and never went away again, had their own kids, and continued the cycle.

My parents were scarcely any different, except come spring they went to Southeast Alaska for a couple of months to fish salmon. I had gone with them from my earliest days right up through high school. I had a sister who had married a fisherman from Sitka. I'm sure my folks would have preferred the situation reversed: my sister and her children living nearby and me hidden away in Sitka.

"I'm here," I called out, going in through the front door. "Right on time."

A small entryway opened onto the living room/dining room, beyond which was the kitchen. It being two minutes past seven my father had abandoned *his* chair; the news being over he had undoubtedly gone to wash up.

"Hello, Michael." My mother came out from the kitchen. She was a sturdy woman who shunned makeup and had let her hair go silver. She wore a simple housedress with a button-up sweater over it and terry-cloth slippers. Reaching up to give me a quick peck on the cheek, she turned and marched back to the kitchen.

Following behind her I went to the refrig and extracted a beer.

"I thought you gave that up," she said. Her blue eyes, deep like the lines in her face from years of fishing, fastened to mine.

"I have, more or less."

"Looks like less to me."

I grinned, held the bottle in the crook of my right arm, and twisted off the cap.

"You still taking those pills?"

I shook my head no as I gulped down a mouthful of beer. "I'm cured."

She turned from the stove and looked at me skeptically. "If you're cured then they must know what was wrong with you."

"It was somethin' I ate."

She resumed her cooking, but suddenly turned and waved

her wooden spoon at me, spilling sauce unnoticed on the floor. "I been doing some reading, Michael, since all this happened to you. They say there's something going around called delayed stress. They say in the next few years there'll be thousands more boys coming down with it."

"Good, I'll look forward to the company."

"It seems to me, Michael, that if so many of you boys . . ."

"Mom, we ain't boys no more. None of us under thirty." I took another swallow of beer. "And I'm not crazy. Warped maybe, but not crazy. What happened out there . . . that was just something that happened. I short-circuited, it could have happened to anyone . . ."

"But it didn't happen to anyone. It happened to you!"

"That's right it did, so you better just accept that your son lost not only his arm in Vietnam but part of his mind too. Fortunately the mind seems to have far greater regenerative powers than the body and it grew back. Now whether it grew back stronger or weaker or just the same with all the original and optional defects remains to be seen. But right now I'm fine, matter-of-fact I'm feeling better than I have in a long while. If I could just get laid everything would be hunky-dory. So I'll thank you to stop watching as if you expected me to start frothing at the mouth any second now."

"Hello, Mike," my father grunted, coming into the kitchen. "Thought you quit drinking?"

"Did. Gave up water." I went into the living room, grabbed *The Sporting News* from beside Pop's chair, and plopped myself down on the couch. The Mariners were on another losing streak. I'd come to appreciate them as much, if not more, than their winning streaks: They were longer, more substantial. Tu had never been to a baseball game. I wanted to take him, but we'd have to wait until fishing season was over.

We were actually very close to being ready now. Food, fuel, and water were the major items on the list, and they could all be had in a day or two. The engine still needed a little work, but the way things stood between Pop and me it looked like I wouldn't be getting much help in that department. I still hadn't checked out the hydraulics, although I thought they were probably in fairly good shape. Then there were the odds and ends, some of which were invariably overlooked. Season opened in a week. We'd just make it.

"Dinner."

My father sat at the head of the table, and I sat at his right, across from my mother, who served us. Her idea of women's lib was that my father brought home the money and what happened to it after that was up to her. They bowed their heads in silence for a moment. Then we dug in. Roast lamb, baked potatoes, fresh asparagus, French bread, sour cream, strawberry preserves. My mother never had learned how to cook for less than eight, which was fine with me as I wouldn't eat so well for months.

The dinner table had never been a place of lively debate in my family, and that night was no exception. If anything was to be said, it would not be before coffee was poured. When the table was cleared, coffee was served with fresh peach pie. Despite being prepared, the opening salvo took me by surprise and immediately lowered my resistance to the ensuing attack.

"I received a card from Leigh Anne the other day," my mother mentioned casually, stirring her coffee, which she drank black.

With the hook I reached for a toothpick from the small crystal container beside the cream pitcher, then speared my gums with the point.

"Please, Michael, don't do that."

"Do what? Clean my teeth, or use the hook?"

"Be civil to your mother, you hear me?"

"What'd Leigh Anne say?" I asked, ignoring my father.

My mother sipped her coffee, making me wait.

"She's still in the Keys. Sounds happy. Asked to be remembered to you."

"Remembered? I'd like to be re-membered all right."

"She's been doing some shrimping. Sounds as if she's got a fella."

Sometimes I thought my mother sat up nights devising cleaner and swifter ways of cutting off my nuts. But I realized it was paranoid of me to think it was intentional when it was purely spontaneous.

Once I'd been thrown off guard by that poison piece of provocation, my father got in a few body punches.

"I hope you're not still thinking of taking that Vietnamese fella fishing."

"Really, Michael, what ever possessed you?" added my mother.

"I don't know," I shrugged, "I thought it was the Christian thing to do."

"Why? Is he a Christian?"

I thought about it for a moment, unsure of what it had to do with anything. "You know, I don't think he ever said. Would it make a difference?"

"Well, I . . ."

I tapped the cream pitcher with the tip of the hook.

"Stop that."

I raised my head and looked up at her. "Tell me, do you think if someone else had taken Tu on, someone who'd never been to Nam, a low-profile sort of a guy, with two hands and no reputation for being wacko, you think there would have been any trouble?"

"What's that got to do with anything?" my father demanded.

"Well, folks just don't want to have anything to do with the guys who went to Vietnam."

"Now that's not true and . . ."

"Let me finish!"

"Michael, you don't have to shout. Your father is not deaf."

"Okay, I'm sorry I shouted, but let me finish what I have to say."

My father turned stone-faced. Looking into the coffee pot, my mother decided it was time for a refill and took it into the kitchen.

"As I was saying"—I spoke loud enough to be heard in the kitchen without shouting—"when the boys this country sent to Vietnam came home ragged old men, nobody would have anything to do with us. When the refugees we created fled to this benevolent land of ours, nobody wanted to have anything to do with them either."

My mother returned with a fresh pot of coffee and poured my father a cup.

"I'm not boring you, am I?"

"No, Michael, not at all. Please continue."

"How 'bout you, Pop?"

"I'm listening."

"Good. If Vietnam vets are painful to look at"—I tapped the cream pitcher to get their attention—"especially if they are disfigured, and Vietnamese refugees are an accusatory presence, then in combination we must be a nightmare."

Both my mother and father held their coffee cups to their faces as if they were porcelain oxygen masks capable of filtering out any harsh, unpleasant realities that might infest their existence.

"Tu and I are a sort of guerrilla theater, or better still, theater of the absurd. How else can this irrational response be accounted for? Do you suppose if someone who had no association with Vietnam, say, one of the Waldrons—good ol' boys through and through—suppose one of them had taken Tu on. Do you think there'd be the row that's goin' on? I don't. I say it would have gone almost unnoticed. But they'd never do it. Only someone half *loon,* like me, with all kinds of associations to Vietnam, would give Tu a chance. So you might say a row was unavoidable. Unless I didn't take him fishing."

"Exactly!" my father insisted, taking his porcelain mask from his face. "If you didn't take this fella fishin' there wouldn't be no problem."

"Wrong! There wouldn't be a problem if you and all the other parents in this country hadn't sent their children to Vietnam."

"Don't say that to your father, Michael. It's not his fault."

"I could have played ball, Pop."

"You weren't that good."

"We were talkin' University of Washington, not the Dodgers. The Huskies wanted me to try out."

"Son, you were good for Everett, but that's where it stopped. You'da been cut. You'da been disappointed. And then you'da been drafted. It was best you went in and got it out of the way."

"Get what out of the way? My arm, my life?"

"Vietnam wasn't our fault, Mike. You're just going to have to accept that."

"Maybe not the *war,* not the whole shootin' match. But you're sure as hell responsible for my part of it. Responsible that I went and for what happened to me." Again I tapped the cream pitcher with the hook.

"That's not our fault," they protested almost in unison. "The Communists did that to you."

"The Communists?" I snarled. "More like the American people. Vietnam was an atrocity. An atrocity perpetrated by the children of this country with the permission of their parents at the direction of the government. As long as you deny that then those of us who fought will forever carry the collective guilt and shame that is Vietnam."

I looked long and hard at their faces, searching for some hint of recognition, but found none.

I pushed away from the table and went to the entry-room closet and pulled on my jacket. Outside it was raining again, straight down, without the hint of a breeze. The fine drops fell across the glow of the streetlamps. I went slowly down the steps of my childhood, the ones I had once tumbled down, chipping a tooth and breaking the wrist I no longer had.

I sat in the cab of the truck, letting the engine warm, smoking a cigarette. As a boy I had stood in this very street playing catch with my father. Every spring night that it didn't rain we'd tossed the ball around, and again in the summer when we returned from Alaska. We never argued. Never argued when we fished either. But now it seemed as if we'd argued all our lives. I would never reconcile with them. It was a lost cause, or no cause at all. Tu would be my family from now on.

CHAPTER 8

Any boat, but especially a work boat, is an endless procession of tasks and chores; if you completed them all before setting forth, you'd spend your life tied up at the dock. But finally, by the time we started laying in stores, I was comfortable with the state that *Leigh Anne* was in.

I bought Tu a set of foul-weather gear and rubber boots. He seemed to think these were the greatest things since his army uniform, and I had to convince him that not only would it not be low profile to wear them to the market—it being one of the few warm, dry days of the spring—it might even be construed as flaunting his presence. He reluctantly agreed. When we headed out to load up on supplies he was dressed as had become his custom: blue running shoes, black Frisco jeans, brown wool plaid shirt, contrasting green wool plaid jacket, and Mariners baseball cap. In other words, just like me, except for the heavy canvas jacket I wore and my leather slip-on fisherman shoes.

We filled two shopping carts. Heavy on the starch—rice,

noodles, cereal, pancake batter, biscuit mix—knowing the protein would be coming in over the gunnels by the ton. Two cases of soda pop, four of beer, one of canned milk, ten pounds of coffee, and two large boxes of tea bags for Tu. Plus the usual condiments: mustard, catsup, ten pounds of sugar, and a zillion cookies.

At the checkout stand we encountered the lovely and voluptuous Miss B. She was all smiles as she ran our prodigious order through her register. In high school she had been the second-best thing to being a cheerleader: She had humped the entire football team. Back then I'd been saving myself, but now . . . now was a different time.

"Four for a dollar, twenty-nine cents each. Goin' fishin', Mike?"

"Sure am, Mary Lou."

"Heard you had a little trouble."

"That so? Where'd you hear a thing like that?"

"You know." she smiled. "Forty-nine cents a pound, three for ninety-nine cents. Talk gets around. Fifty-five cents six times."

"It surely does, doesn't it?"

"You gonna be the highliner this year? Eleven-eighty-eight a case."

"Why, of course. Who'd you expect?"

"Seventy-eight twice. Well, Pete McGuire has been the last couple of years."

"Good ol' Pete. How is he? Haven't seen him in ages."

"Oh, I ain't hardly seen him either. That's one hundred eighty-eight dollars and forty-four cents. Out of two hundred. So when you headin' out, Mike?"

"Tomorrow. Early."

"Your change is eleven-fifty-six. Stop on by later and I'll fix you a drink."

"Well now, I may just do that."

Tu and I pushed our carts out to the truck and loaded up.

"I think this woman, she likes you?"

"Likes me?" I laughed. "All she likes, partner, is the old ranger."

"Old ranger? Who is this?"

I put my hand to my crotch and rearranged it with a grin. "This, my friend, is the old ranger."

For a moment I thought Tu might actually blush, but he held on and forced a grin and a small laugh.

We laid in the supplies that afternoon and that night I laid in Miss B. It was a relief, in more ways than one. It's not good to go off fishing, or on any long journey where there are no women, without getting laid one last time. Even a week before leaving is too long time, because you go off thinking you haven't been laid for a while when you could have been, and that's what you carry with you. But getting laid at the last possible moment leaves you with the feeling that you're sexual, have used your sex fully, and that the weeks and months of celibacy ahead are externally imposed and therefore more tolerable. All of which was patently absurd as I hadn't been laid in months.

Miss B. was the most delightfully horny woman I have known. She emanated the male fantasy of sex without responsibility. The good whore, promising guilt-free, entanglement-free sex and all the emptiness that goes along with it. Nevertheless it was a rambunctious fuck that left me feeling pleased that I could still do it without it turning to mayhem.

When I departed her place I decided to cruise the Riptide. I hadn't stopped in since *Leigh Anne* had been defaced, and it wouldn't do to go off fishing without having made an appearance. Even though I wasn't intimidated it might look like I was, and that only encouraged folks.

Parked out front was a pickup I recognized. Circling the block I thought over what I might expect from an encounter with the truck's owner. I had a fairly good idea of who it was that had been involved in the vandalizing of my boat. Most of them were no-account fishermen, hadn't fished long; their fathers were loggers or worked at Boeing. All but one: Pete McGuire. He was as local as they come, and it was his pickup I'd seen.

When I pulled around in front of the tavern again there was a space beside McGuire's truck, and I pulled the Power Wagon in alongside. Like mine, his was a family of fishermen; both our fathers had fished in Southeast Alaska and Bristol Bay. I also suspected they'd both courted my mother, although I didn't know that for a fact. But whenever my father bad-mouthed McGuire's father my mother would stick up for him, if only by her silence. There was no less love lost between Pete's father and mine than there was between Pete and me. He and I had played on rival Little League teams; he used to strike me out about half the time, and the other half I'd hit home runs off him. During Vietnam he'd drawn a lottery number in the three-hundreds and never looked back.

McGuire was sitting at the bar with his back to the door. He was shorter than me and thicker. He wore a blue-and-white baseball cap low over his eyes. His hair was red and his beard was like brick. Beside him sat his deckhand, a young guy who thought himself pretty tough but wasn't.

At the corner table sat three other fishermen. They were the ones, along with Pete and his deckhand, whom I suspected of having terrorized Tu and my boat. In back a couple of women were ripping felt on one of the pool tables.

I went up to the bar and stood tight between McGuire's deckhand and the next stool and ordered a beer. The deckhand tried to spread himself out and get back some of the room I'd pinched, but when I put the hook up on the bar beside him he shrank back. I paid for my beer and turned to McGuire, speaking right past the nose of his deckhand.

"Evening, Pete."

"Mike. How are you?"

"Good, Pete. How 'bout yourself?"

"Can't kick."

He looked up and held his gaze on me. His blue eyes set deep under the bill of his cap and his thick red eyebrows.

"Ain't seen you about for a while," he said, cordial enough.

"Been gettin' ready for the season. Had some unexpected repairs to do on the boat this year."

"That so?"

I turned sideways to the bar. At the corner table the rest of the riffraff were intently watching the goings-on. I raised the hook to them and waved. They didn't wave back.

"So what brings you out tonight, Mike?"

"Payin' my respects to the ladies . . ."

"Still paying for it are you?" the deckhand chuckled, looking to his skipper for approval.

McGuire grunted. "Pull up a stool, Mike."

"Thanks, I will." I put down my beer and leaned my face close to the deckhand. "You're sitting in my seat, asshole."

"The fuck I am."

I caught the lobe of his ear in the tines of the hook and cranked down on it. He came up off his stool and I lifted his beer and walked him over to the table where his friends sat. He joined them gladly, and I turned back to the bar and took up the vacated stool.

"What do you think of the season, Pete?" I asked, lighting a cigarette.

"Shorter and shorter every year," he answered, looking up to meet my reflection in the mirror behind the bar. "Soon there won't be a trolling season. Goddamn foreigners trying to worm their way into the fleet. Indians getting half the catch in the Sound."

"I suppose that's what the Indians think."

"What?"

"That we're a buncha foreigners the government gave half their fish to."

"Shit. I say catch as catch can and damn some hundred-year-old treaty."

"Every man for himself?"

"Hell yes."

"That include foreigners?"

His eyes drifted up from his beer to meet mine in the mirror.

"You remember that game," I asked, changing the subject, "in Little League? I think it was either the last game of the season or maybe a play-off game."

"It was a play-off. We ended the season tied for first."

"That's right. You were pitching and there was a big fight between your dad and mine over some technicality. You remember that? What was it?"

He laughed. "Yeah, I remember. Each pitcher could only pitch so many innings a week, and your old man was all bent outta shape 'cause I'd already pitched a full game that week, but that was regular season and we were in the play-offs.''

"But just like basketball, if you go into overtime you keep your fouls and you don't get anymore.''

"It was a new game, it wasn't overtime. The ump ruled in favor of us, and I kept pitching.''

"That's right.'' I nodded. "We played under protest, but it didn't matter 'cause in the last inning I wacked a triple off you with the bases loaded and we won by a run.''

"Big fucking deal. That was twenty years ago. What do you do, lay awake at night thinking about your one big moment of glory?''

I shook my head. "No. I'm just using it to make a point. You can stack the deck in your favor and fuck with me all you want, Pete, but in the end I'm going to beat you. So, why don't you make it easy on yourself, and me, and leave things be? That way won't neither of us get hurt. 'Cause if you fuck with me I guarantee you'll come out the worst for it.'' I tapped my glass with the hook. "You got more to lose than me.''

"You're the loser, Randel. You lost the war. You lost your arm. And you lost your wife. Me, I'm a highliner. If I'd gone to Vietnam we'da won. And if you and that Vietnamese slope go out on the fishing grounds I'll kick your ass.''

"I didn't see you volunteering for the draft, Pete. Come after me out there and I'll give you a little taste of what you missed in Vietnam; I'll cut your balls off.''

I turned from the bar and headed toward the door. "Night, boys.'' I waved the hook at the deckhand and the assortment of punks seated with him.

Outside it was raining. I started up the Power Wagon. Turning the wheel sharply, I eased the clutch until my bumper came to rest against the side panel of McGuire's *foreign* pickup. I gunned the engine long and loud till I saw McGuire's face appear in the tavern window. I played with the clutch, letting the truck rock back and forth, the engine whining, McGuire's eyes bugging in my headlights. Then I slowly eased the clutch, and the bumper of the Power Wagon creased the side of his little truck from stem to stern.

CHAPTER 9

We were neither the first to leave that morning nor the last. Up and down the Sound trollers were on the move, headed for the Strait and west to the coast for the opening of salmon season. First light was still a ways off, and we were running on depth-sounder and radar. Slack tide would soon be followed by a strong ebb whisking us around to Port Angeles by midday.

I loved to run at night. The wheelhouse, dimly lit by the shining faces of the electronics, was my conning tower, a haven, a womb where I was insulated from the world. The old diesel Jimmy went *chug-chug-chug,* and the radar screen swept the night, showing our way clear.

Tu was fascinated by the electronics, never having seen them in operation at night. I explained the depth-sounder to him, the radar he seemed to understand, and the large compass, lit red, he was on intimate terms with. He had finally learned how to brew a decent pot of coffee—although he only drank tea—and after he poured me a mugful I gave him a heading and let him take the wheel.

I stepped out onto the deck with my coffee and a cigarette. I took a deep breath of diesel and damp salt air. The lights of Everett, muted in the mist, receded in our wake as we headed down Possession Sound. It felt strange to be starting a new season without Leigh Anne, not unlike reaching for something with my right arm only to discover once more that my hand was gone.

Leigh Anne and I never did get to Hawaii. A little plot on the Big Island had been our dream. A small house with a large garden, papaya and banana. The money had not been good our second season, although it had been a considerable improvement over the first. I had toyed with the idea of going crabbing in Alaska that winter—a demented idea, I discovered just in time—but by then Leigh Anne had already left for Florida, where her parents were wintering. It was a month before I let her know I was still in Everett. I was sober very little that month; spent my first night in jail. They took away the hook.

When Leigh Anne learned I had not gone to Alaska she was livid. Why I don't know. She had insisted I not go in the first place. We could have used the money, but it would have been suicidal (crabbing in the Bering Sea is high-risk business even with two hands).

I did go out with my old buddy Alan on his boat, *Talisman,* and fish dogs. We didn't make any money, but then we didn't lose any either. Just went out for a day or two at a shot, drinking beer in the rain, killing time.

Leigh Anne stayed in Florida. She was making money she said, in the Keys, fishing. I kept drinking, gave up writing to her. Began to think I might not see her again. Not for any particular reason; just because.

Alan hooked up with some hippie chick who wore thongs even in the rain and said "Wow" a lot. She made Leigh Anne look calm, and I couldn't take being around her. I developed a passion for science fiction and took to hanging out by myself on *Leigh Anne,* drinking beer and reading. I'd sit with my feet wedged in the spokes of the wheel, the afghan Leigh Anne had crocheted for our bed draped over my shoulders, sci-fi in hand, Rainier and Camels within reach.

It wasn't a bad time; a little lonely, a little boring, but not bad. Except for my weekly visit to my folks for dinner and laundry it was a peaceful existence. There was hardly a soul on my dock, it being exclusively fishing boats and the season over.

Then one afternoon she was there. I had just entered "the outer parsac of the transgalatic nebula 91C" when I reached for a sip of Rainier and saw her heading down the float toward me.

It was gray out and misting. Her head was down slightly and the bill of her marlin fishing cap—a transparent green—was pulled low. I could just barely see her face—*a* face, for I could not see enough detail, except in my mind's eye, to say that it was hers—but there was no doubt that it was. Her hair was down about her shoulders and she wore her ever-present Birkenstocks and wool socks, jeans, wool jacket, shoulder bag, hands snuggled deep inside her pockets.

It was her walk that immediately recalled everything about her that I loved, and that which I despised myself for hating. Here was her irrepressible spirit, bounding uncontrollably in every nook and cranny of her person as her long legs propelled her along the dock in a kinetic lope that moved her as much up and down as forward. It was this that I loved, longed for, yet hated because it mocked my pain, disavowed my suffering.

Why was she here? She who had never had a hard decision in her life, had never experienced pain or seen suffering. She who loved life and saw only its unending possibilities, as if there were no limitations, no restraints, only new adventures and undiscovered pleasures.

I hated all that she loved because I could not have it. I knew that to despise beauty, to destroy love, to defile purity, was a crime. A hideous, unforgivable crime, worse than any I had committed in Vietnam, for it was committed with forethought, malice, and a consenting—if somewhat disturbed—mind.

Yet I could not restrain myself. I could not at the last moment, before she looked up from beneath her impossibly long green-billed cap, with her silly mischievous grin, throw open the wheelhouse door and warn her off. Yell at her to go, to run and never look back, to save herself, and me, before it was too late.

It was almost slack water. *Leigh Anne* moved through the flat sea at a steady six knots. I flicked the butt of my cigarette into the night and stepped back into the mute electronic glow of the wheelhouse.

"Tu, did you ever stand guard at night, during the war?"

He laughed. "When did I not stand guard at night?" he replied.

"Working on your sarcasm I see."

"I am getting it better?"

"Yes, you are getting it better. Before long you'll be sarcastic right up there with the best of them."

"It is American way, yes?"

"Knock it off, you sound like a parrot."

"What is parrot?"

"It's a bird. A painted bird that talks."

"Birds do not talk, Mike."

"Look, who's the captain of this ship? If I say birds talk then birds talk. How'd we get on this subject? Standing guard at night. Jesus, we've only been out for an hour and already we're making loose associations."

"What is this?"

"Loose association?"

"Yes."

"If I'm talking about Vietnam and then suddenly start talking about the price of cabbage . . ."

"What does this have to do with Vietnam?"

"Exactly. That's what I mean. That's a loose association."

He took his eyes from the compass and looked up at me. "This makes no sense."

"Right. Now you got it." I laughed. "Loose associations make no sense. You and me, we're a loose association. Very loose. We make no sense whatsoever."

Tu turned back to the compass. "It is so, I fear."

I was at the helm when dawn came and we rounded Possession Point, well out from the buoy with its shoal warning. Skirting the light at Scatchet Head we crossed Useless Bay and

continued on up the west side of Whidbey Island. We were
with the ebb and moving well. Trollers that we had seen only
as running lights and dots on the radar screen came slowly into
focus before and behind. As we passed into Admiralty Inlet,
above Foulweather Bluff and the mouth of the Hood Canal,
still others joined us. The hunters were gathering.

Finally Port Townsend fell behind, and then we were around
Point Wilson and into the Strait of Juan de Fuca. To the north
the San Juan Islands were, as always, lost in a heavy shroud of
damp fog. The Strait was calm, open.

I had not been below deck for five minutes when Tu started
yelling. Barreling up the companionway I almost knocked myself unconscious on a low deck beam. "What? What is it?" I
demanded, reeling into the wheelhouse. Looking around I could
see nothing: no tankers about to run us over, no rocks rising
suddenly before us.

Tu was wide-eyed, pointing frantically out the window at the
flat sea before us. "Look, look, look!" He kept yelling.

And then a fin cut the surface and continued to rise to the
fantastic height of almost five feet before the black behemoth it
was attached to began to show and its white saddle patch came
into view. It was a bull killer whale and beside it rose another
and another and still another. There were almost a dozen of
them, mostly females, but here and there a young one showed
and two more males trailed behind.

I started to laugh, rubbed my aching head, and slapped Tu
on the shoulder. "Whales!" I told him. "Very big fish."

"Fish?" he said, incredulous.

"Well, sort of. Mammals." I threw Iron Mike, the autopilot,
into gear and took Tu out on deck. They were abeam of us now
and moving off. They paid us no mind, rising and blowing,
sinking beneath the surface, rising again. Slick and smooth, in-
domitable black-and-white squad cars, top predators of the deep
blue. Water slid from their backs as they arched effortlessly to
partake of that which they could neither live in nor without.

Tu remained paralyzed as our visitors moved off into the recesses of the gray dawn.

"Whales."

He nodded his head. "Whales."

"Mammals. You *bic* mammals?"

He turned to me angrily. "I not Coke-boy, Cap'n Mike. Speak pretty good English."

"Sorry. You're right. I apologize."

Tu returned to the wheelhouse without further comment, and I went below to find the coffee boiling. I threw it out and started over, mixed up a bunch of pancakes and fried bacon. When I had eaten my fill I fixed Tu a plate of the same and carried it up to the wheelhouse. I took the helm, and he stood beside me to eat.

We stayed well out from Dungeness Spit and the tall white lighthouse tower that stood at the tip. Broken patches of snow and ice clinging to the flanks of the Olympic Mountains showed through the low clouds. Port Angeles was not far beyond. It would be a fast run.

"What rank were you in the army, Tu?"

"Cap'n," he said bluntly.

"That so?" I replied, trying to contain my surprise. What had I thought? He had been a career soldier, a lifer. So why did I think of him as a private? Or did I really mean a peasant? Were my prejudices so deeply rooted that when all was said and done I could only see him in shorts and a conical straw hat pushing a plow through a rice paddy behind a water buffalo? A Stone Age peasant whose immutable Oriental stare said nothing but told everything? Prejudices die hard.

"Captain Tu," I started to say.

"Please, no cap'n. That is past. Call me Tu."

I sipped my coffee and lit a cigarette, uncomfortable at the gap that suddenly looked so much larger and more difficult to span than I had naïvely assumed it to be.

"Then you must call me Mike."

"But you are cap'n of this boat."

"It doesn't matter. I want you to call me Mike from now on. Okay?"

"Okay, Mike."

"Good. Now, getting back to whales. Do you understand what mammals are?"

"I do not know the word. Maybe I understand its meaning if you tell me."

"Okay. The definition of a mammal is something like: warm-blooded, breathes air, gives birth to live babies—you know, not eggs, but living whalies—and the babies suckle milk from their mother's tit, breasts, mammaries. That's it! Mammals have mammaries. You understand mammaries?" I cupped my hands in front of my chest as if I were cradling a pair of melons. "Bosoms, breasts, tits, knockers, mammaries."

Tu grinned and nodded his head. "Mammaries?"

"That's right. Whales, women, and water buffalo all have mammaries. All mammals."

"Whales, women, and water buffalo?" He laughed and shook his head. "And fish?"

"No! No mammaries. Fish don't have tits."

"Fish don't have tits. Okay, Mike."

"Good. Glad we got that straightened out."

10

CHAPTER

Inexplicably I began to feel gray and washed out, as lacking in texture and warmth as the day. It was not depression so much as despondency that lowered its pall from time to time. Seemingly without reason, or warning, it would be upon me, as if on a warm and peaceful day a wave suddenly broke across the bow, soaking me in its cold spray, leaving me chilled and dazed.

I didn't know where to begin to put the blame, if *blame* was the right word. If it just *was*, without blame, then what did I do with it? Embrace it? Reject it? Ignore it? I had done all of those things and still it was there.

"Do you ever miss the war?"

"No."

Startled to hear Tu's voice, I realized that what I thought I'd asked of myself I had actually said out loud. He peered out the wheelhouse windows, over the bow at the flat gray water that mingled with the smoky gray sky.

"I miss my country, my people. My family buried there. War

sometimes must be and then must be endured, but it not something to be missed."

"I don't believe you. You were a warrior, Tu. You became a soldier when you were a boy and you fought all your life. How old are you?"

"Forty-eight."

"Did you join the army? Were you drafted? How'd you become an officer? ROTC?"

"It was not so simple as to be drafted. I live with my grandparents and mother and my aunts and sisters. This was near to the finish of World War Two. My uncle, his sons, and my older brother are fighting against the Japanese and always the French. I began when I am very young to work for the Vietminh as a messenger."

I would be hard pressed to call it a blinding flash of insight, considering the time Tu and I had already spent together, but my keen mind—moving constantly at the terminal velocity of a desert slug—was suddenly overwhelmed with a formerly unrecognized possibility. "Where were you born?"

"Haiphong," he answered without hesitation.

"That's near Hanoi, isn't it?"

"Eighty-five kilometers."

"Well within the boundary of North Vietnam, wouldn't you say?"

"There are never two Vietnams. But yes, Haiphong is in the North."

I shook my head in disbelief. "Just who were you a captain with, Tu? You weren't ARVN, were you?"

"I never say this."

"Fuckin' NVA. I can't believe it!" I burst out laughing. "My deckhand was with the North fuckin' Vietnamese Army!"

Tu said nothing. He stared straight ahead, keeping *Leigh Anne* to her course.

As we cruised inside of Ediz Hook, which defines the harbor at Port Angeles, and made for the dock, I saw that scores and scores of trollers had already gathered. Their bare trolling poles—a forest of burned-over saplings—were a sight to behold. Like an airstrip full of choppers, or the players standing shoulder to shoulder along the foul lines at the start of the World Series, action was imminent.

Once inside the harbor we rafted up beside another troller, and without a word to Tu I went in search of a tavern.

The pool tables were in use, and the bar was littered with local drunks and transient fishermen spending the afternoon in varying degrees of intoxication. I pushed my baseball cap back on my head, held a cigarette in the hook, and began to drink. The cold brew went down easy and in no time I'd polished off two or three, my head of steam turning slowly to foam.

I contemplated what difference it made to me that Tu was North Vietnamese. Did I really care, or was I just startled? NVA. Goddamn, I couldn't believe it. Maybe he'd been the one who'd fired the rocket that knocked my chopper out of the sky. Why had he been thrown out of his country? Had he even been thrown out or had he escaped? Why would a career officer want to escape just when his side won final victory?

"Vietnamese." The word entered my mind from somewhere. I looked down the bar and saw a fellow with his back to me gulp his beer then lower it and say, "Cut the boat loose and pushed him away . . ."

I went out the door on the run, dodged a honking car, skidded on the wet street and almost went down. A couple of fishermen I vaguely recognized were walking up from the dock talking loudly and flourishing their arms. I saw them turn as I ran past, heard my name.

As soon as I hit the floats I saw *Leigh Anne* cruising slowly back and forth, just off from where we had tied up. She looked strangely frail, like a child in over its head trying desperately to get to the side of the pool. Four men armed with boat hooks moved along the outer row of trollers. As *Leigh Anne* motored back and forth, her assailants moved with her. Jumping awkwardly from one boat to the next with their long-hooked poles they kept her at bay.

Clusters of boaters and fishermen stood about gawking. I ran along the outer float trying to get Tu's attention without alerting his attackers. I could not see him in the wheelhouse, could only hope that he was on the lookout for me.

It was Pete McGuire and his boys, as I knew it would be. They were too busy with their dirty work to notice me. As Tu motored *Leigh Anne* slowly along the dock, McGuire and company boat-hopped along with him. Quickly working my way out to the final row of boats I came up behind McGuire's deckhand, who was farthest from *Leigh Anne*. When Tu turned once again and headed our way, I stepped up behind the deckhand and coldcocked him. He went into the water, and I waved my arms frantically to get Tu's attention. When McGuire and the others saw what had happened, they came down the line of boats as fast as they could. I jumped to the next boat and stood in the bow and again waved my arms. *Leigh Anne* suddenly picked up speed. Tu had spotted me. I scampered from boat to boat, managing to keep ahead of McGuire and his boys by a couple of lengths.

Tu maneuvered *Leigh Anne* expertly up alongside, slowing slightly as I stepped out, grabbed the starboard trolling pole, and swung aboard. Tu upped the revs and we pulled away. I went aft to wave good-bye. Pete stood defiant, boat hook straight up at his side like a spear, hat pulled low over his eyes, red beard flowing. I knew only too well it would not end here.

"We're having some kinda fun now," I said to my NVA comrade as I stepped into the wheelhouse.

He studied me for a moment but made no reply.

We motored out around the Hook and west along the shore to Freshwater Bay at the mouth of the Elwha River. There we anchored up for the night. It wasn't great protection, but the radio called for fair weather. We were alone with the mountains rising up behind us into the low gray sky and the giant fir trees lining the shore.

Below deck, dinner downed, Tu and I sat nursing our beers. I was honing an edge on my switchblade (being one-handed I could legally carry one), Tu was absently flipping through his English grammar. The stove had turned the galley into a sauna, and we sat at the nook in our T-shirts. While I was still in my jeans, Tu was down to his jockey shorts. This seemed to be his after-hours dress: T-shirt tucked into his jockey shorts and flip-flops on his feet.

He had long, thin legs with calves that jumped out like bricks.

The outside of his right thigh showed a splatter of scar tissue. I had seen it on a number of occasions, but we had never spoken of it. I took it to be a shrapnel wound and the cause of his slight limp, but like I said he didn't mention it and I didn't ask.

Tu and I had done battle together now, had fought a common enemy, but it made me feel even more cut off and isolated from what I knew, who I knew. Looking across the table into his liquid brown eyes, half covered by his droopy lids, I couldn't help but feel I had no complaints when it came to being cut off. Tu was without family, culture, country. But like everything, I suppose, it was a matter of degree. My family had all but disavowed me, my culture was all around me, but I felt mostly as if I lived in a glass booth breathing my own rarefied (or was it putrefied?) air. And as for my country, they had long ago used, abused, and discarded me, same as Tu's.

"Can we talk about Vietnam?" I said.

"What else is there to talk of?"

"We could talk about the price of salmon."

"Would that not be a loose association?"

I burst out laughing. "Great! That was great!"

Tu was abashed. "This is not correct?"

"Yes, yes. It is most correct."

"Then why do you laugh?"

I wiped the tears from my eyes. "Well . . . it's just the way you said it. No, not the way, but that you said it. That you remembered the expression and how you used it." I shook my head. "Humor must be the hardest thing to learn about a new culture."

"Yes, I believe this is true. Americans laugh very much when people hurt themselves. Many things I do not understand about American humor."

I shrugged. "I guess it's just another way of looking at life." He seemed less than satisfied with my answer. "So tell me about Haiphong."

"No baseball," he said with a straight face. Then he grinned. "This is humor, yes?"

I nodded. "Yes. This is humor."

"Good." He lit himself a cigarette. "For me Haiphong very good when I am boy. My father small merchant, second-generation Vietnamese, born in Hanoi. His father Chinese. My mother Vietnamese. China and Vietnam have long history of animosity. What happens now between us is not new. My father was thought of as Chinese, but he always saw himself as Vietnamese.

"Chinese in Vietnam like Jew in America, or Indian in Africa. Why these people became merchants I not know. They make more money than native peoples, their children go more school and make more money. In time they look to be privileged class.

"My father died when I am young, and I do not know what he thought, but I believe him to be bourgeois."

"You don't believe in free enterprise?"

"I not believe one person should grow rich off labor of another. Do you?"

"This is my boat. You're working for me and I'm paying you ten percent of the catch. Do you think it'd be fair if we split fifty-fifty? I paid for the boat. And it took me a lot of time and hard work to learn how to catch fish."

"I most satisfied with ten percent, Cap'n Mike."

"That's not what I'm asking you."

"I am sure you worked hard for this boat. I do not believe you exploited the masses"—he grinned shyly—"in order to obtain it. You own the means of production. I am honored to share a small portion with you."

"Okay, okay." I took a sip of warm beer.

"Beside, I am the son of capitalist." His grin grew broader.

"You're not a Communist?" I could feel my eyes squinting, the bottle in my hand felt like a gavel, and I could see myself leaning down from the bench to stare at the accused. *Are you now, or have you ever been . . .*

"Why is this word so . . ." He hesitated, pondering. "So explosive?" He looked at me closely. "I see it all time in American newspaper and TV. It is talked of like sickness. It is only a way for all peoples to share wealth of country. Is this not democratic?"

I shrugged. "Beats me. I don't really give a shit. As long as I can fish and make a living for myself, that's all I care about."

"This is the American way?"

I studied his face, trying to see if this was more of the beginnings of his sense of humor, or even sarcasm, but he seemed dead serious. "Yes. It's the American way. Take what you can get and fuck everyone else."

"This man with beard." Tu touched his chin. "McGuire? He thinks if I fish other Vietnamese will come and there will be not enough for him? This is so?"

"This is so."

"You think so too?"

I nodded. "Could be."

"Then why do you fish with me?"

"I don't. You fish with me. And I'll take anyone fishing I damn well please. That's the American way."

CHAPTER 11

Crouched in the bow of the Olympic Peninsula, just east of where Cape Flattery juts defiantly into the confluence of the Strait of Juan de Fuca and the Pacific Ocean, lies Neah Bay, a rain-soddened, wind-blown little fishing village. The mighty forces of wind, sea, and land are much in evidence there. The thick stub of the Olympic Mountains rides the back of the Peninsula like a giant spiny barnacle, spurring the cape farther and farther into the relentless grinding gears of the Pacific and the Strait. Pressed between the Peninsula and Vancouver Island to the north, the Pacific squeezes into the Strait, stacking up waves and chewing at the shore and those foolish enough to venture forth. It is a spectacular place, full of power and mystery, gray, wet, and miserable. I loved it!

Tu and I arrived in a drizzle just before noon. A westerly had made for a sloppy ride as it blew counter to the ebb. Rock and tree stood like ghosts in the mist along the shore. I was tired. I had not slept well, and I was generally pissed at the world.

Fishing season opened in two days, and instead of looking forward to it I was looking back over my shoulder.

The immediate problem was what to do for the night; our friends would certainly arrive sometime that day. We could move on, anchor off Mushroom Rock, even turn the corner at Cape Flattery and slide down the coast to La Push. But Neah Bay was where I wanted to be; and I could not avoid McGuire all season.

We pulled in at the cannery dock and iced the fishhold. Then we moved around to the main dock and rafted up beside a boat from Bellingham. The skipper helped us tie up and didn't stare at my hook or my deckhand.

From the locker in the wheelhouse I removed and assembled the .22, dug out the box of .22 longs, and handed the works to Tu. "Go ahead," I told him, "load it."

He dropped the shiny little bullets one at a time down the loading chamber. I could see him squatting in the jungle, the consummate wilderness survivor: Ho Chi Minh camp stove, AK-47, black PJs. I left him to his task and went in search of our needs.

I turned up my collar and pulled low the brim of my Mariners cap. I mused that it would be truly magnanimous of the gods to give us a break in the weather for the opening, but it seemed unlikely. Tomorrow, or the following day, we would make the six- or seven-hour run out to the Prairie—an area off the coast where the sea floor came up abruptly from two hundred fathoms to sixty and the fishing could be excellent.

I found the things I needed: extra hoochies, flashers, plugs, and swivels, length of hydraulic hose, and fuel filters. Items that caused me to wonder at my lack of preparedness. "Don't let the first thing go wrong" was Pop Randel's motto. It was the only way to be safe, for if the first thing never went wrong, then neither did the second or third. I was suspiciously close to letting the first thing go wrong simply by being shy the few extras I hadn't bothered to pick up. I'd taken care of the major things, but it was always the little things that gave out when you least expected it, or most expected it and least needed it to.

I bought some more groceries and stumbled down the road

with a large shopping bag under each arm. I tried not to think of the previous year, when Leigh Anne and I had made the same walk, laughing as we headed back to the boat and an afternoon of lovemaking.

She and I had played a game where I would undress her with the hook. When we first became lovers she wouldn't let me wear the hook to bed; it frightened her. Besides, she was obsessed with the stump. (I think she felt guilty about it.) She would press my truncated arm to her breast, or hold it down between her thighs, as if by doing so she might give birth to a new hand.

But time with the stump dulls its powers of good or evil; it was just a short arm that grew no fingers. As I had, she learned to accept it. Sometimes it pained her, more often it pained me. We called it "the stump" or "thumper" or "the blunt instrument," much as we called my prosthesis "the hook," or my penis "Mr. Dick" or "thumper two," as if each had a life of its own and was not part of the whole.

Initially, Leigh Anne had sensed a certain danger to the hook, as she had me. In time she thrilled to its touch; the arc, rubbed along her leg, excited. I played the pirate, she the reluctant virgin. At first there was no pain, only the eroticism of the forbidden, the excitement of being naughty: the hook sliding the straps of her bra from her shoulders, sliding about the edge of her panties, lowering them with each move until they fell to her ankles. Submissive, she feigned fright, quivered to my dominance, suppressed her giggles, spread herself before me.

That second season of fishing there was seldom sex without the hook. It is difficult to think back on it now without judgment. It wasn't sick, not then at least. Perverted? Well, certainly it was different, aberrant, if only because so few possessed the hook. But the real change was that frustration and anger of a nonsexual nature became the driving force in our lovemaking. Seldom was tenderness involved, although it did creep in on occasion, if significant anger had been exorcised.

I'm tempted to say that there was a decided lack of communication between us, but I think to say so would deny the evidence. Certainly I did not, could not, verbalize my true feelings.

What communication there was consisted of hard, pounding anger. And it was the same message over and over: I was the master, Leigh Anne was the slave; I had the power, she had none. But we both knew that it was only because she let me. And in submitting to me she dominated me, and I grew to hate her for it.

I snorted Neah Bay's highly moisturized air and did as the Scots must do: pretended that sun and warmth are not a condition God wished upon the white man, that low latitudes and lower aptitudes go together, and that webbed feet are a sign of higher evolutionary status.

As I made the rise above the docks I was dismayed to see that a small crowd had gathered about the *Leigh Anne*. Tu was on deck with the .22, clearly engaged in some sort of confrontation. I rushed forward, trying not to spill our supplies.

"What's wrong?" I demanded, elbowing through the throng.

"This fucking Chinaman won't let anyone tie up to him," someone answered.

"Here's the skipper!" hollered the fellow off the boat from Bellingham.

The crowd turned their attention on me.

"Asshole!" someone yelled.

"What the fuck you lettin' foreigners into the fleet for?" called another.

"And who are you, Kawalski? Let me through!" I made it onto the deck of the *Leigh Anne*. "Put the rifle away." I dropped the groceries in the wheelhouse and started up the engine.

Just beyond us was a boat waiting to tie up. The skipper was out on deck looking plenty pissed. I had Tu cast us off. We were wedged between a couple of boats on either end and it took a bit of maneuvering and the assistance of the skipper from Bellingham and his deckhand to free us up. I went out on deck and thanked him as we started to pull away.

"Sorry for the hassle. We've been having a lot of trouble with guys trying to stop us from fishing together. They already tried to burn me out."

"That so?" he replied. His eyes moved to Tu. "He a refugee? Vietnamese?"

I nodded.

He saw my combat badge, still pinned to my jacket. "You a vet?"

"Yeah. You?"

He nodded.

"Get this." I jerked my thumb at Tu. "NVA regular, thirty-five years." My laugh came out sounding kind of crazed.

"You're fucking nuts, man."

I gave him the hook, went to the wheelhouse, spun the wheel, and throttled up. We moved out into the harbor and dropped anchor. I was actually pleased with what had happened. No harm had been done and notice had been served that we were not to be fucked with. The word would spread.

"It was incorrect, my action this afternoon?" Tu had been particularly quiet since his "action" earlier in the day. He sat pensively in the eating nook while I cooked supper.

"Hell no! You did great. You now have a reputation for not taking any shit off anyone."

"I think a reputation is not something to pride."

I looked over my shoulder at him as he stared gloomily into his coffee. "What's wrong, ol' buddy?"

"Cap'n Mike, since I know you I have been shooted at, men try set fire to boat, attack again yesterday, and today I must use weapon to defend myself, perhaps incorrectly. I cannot tell who is friend, who is enemy."

"Yeah? That's just how I felt in Vietnam."

"I did not ask to come here. I was forced from my own country, by mistake." His voice rose in anger.

"Bullshit! It weren't no mistake. They didn't want you. You're Chinese. The revolution used you. When they'd gotten what they wanted from you they threw you out."

"No!" He slammed his hand down on the table. "This not so! It was mistake. All my life I fought for the people, for my people, for Vietnamese peoples. I am Vietnamese, not Chinese."

"Why do you think that after being a soldier for thirty-five years you were just a captain? You musta been the oldest captain in the NVA. Why was that?" When he didn't answer, I said, "I'll tell you, it's 'cause you're Chinese."

"No! It is not so!" Rage came to his face. "Others more deserving."

I laughed. "Sure. And how many of those were Chinese?"

He flew up the companionway and out onto the deck. I moved the skillet to the side of the stove top and went after him. Outside it was black. A light rain was falling and a fresh wind was up from the west. Tu stood in the stern beneath the overhead protection of the skiff.

"I think I cannot fish with you, Mike."

"Well, what the hell do you think you're going to do? Sweep out the Red Dragon for the rest of your life? Right here is the best chance you've got, maybe the only one. Think what you like: that you didn't make major because you weren't smart enough, that for the greater good of the people you did what you had to, and that it really was a mistake that you were thrown out. It doesn't much matter. For better or worse you're in the good ol' U.S. of A., and you're here to stay.

"It's a country that only likes folks who fit the norm: white middle-class Christians with two arms, a regular family, and a job. No Oriental black Jews need apply. Americans don't like extremes of color, politics, religion, thought, or money. This is a profoundly middle-of-the-road, conservative country. Assholes like Pete McGuire abound; they'll push you as far as they can. You don't have to be like 'em to survive, but if you let 'em get the best of you then you never will. Now come eat your pork chops before they dry out."

CHAPTER 12

Dawn. I peered through the windows of the wheelhouse. The weather was no different than it had been at midnight. Only psychopaths would fish this day; I didn't qualify. The swell rolling in the Strait from the Pacific surged loudly against the breakwater, showing white along its length. The rigging of score upon score of trollers was an auditory hallucination: wind chimes gone mad. Rain came in intermittent bursts, beating against the fishing fleet like machine-gun fire.

Leigh Anne was one of very few boats riding alone. The others were rafted up in twos, threes, and fours. Had our reputation spread so fast? Tu had been right when he said that a reputation was not to be cherished. Better to blend in, go unnoticed; that way you could count on help when the need arose. And it always did. The chill wind chased me below to reconvene my sleep in the warmth of my berth.

Later that day I taught Tu to play gin rummy. We played Hollywood gin—that's what my grandmother had called it when she taught me—three column, down with ten or less, twenty points for gin. Excluding war it was Tu's introduction to competitive sports. First set I blanked him; second set he won a game; third, two. At that rate he'd have owned the boat by day's end. Claiming I was tired, I quit.

Tu continued to study his English grammar and his American history. So much of our history paralleled that of his own country, he said to me again and again. America had been an English colony; why had we not responded when Vietnam, as a French colony, had asked for help in her struggle for independence? With the fall of Japan at the end of World War II, Ho Chi Minh had set up a provisional government and pleaded for recognition. But the United States had stalled, thereby giving the French tacit approval to return. This they did with great brutality, bombarding Tu's home, Haiphong, and killing six thousand people.

Tu remained bewildered by this. He saw it as the crossroad that had sealed his fate and steered his life to its present destination: a small fishing village on the northwest tip of the United States, his archenemy, on a fishing boat with a skipper whose sanity he suspected and whose mechanical arm daily called to mind that this man had fought against and killed his people. It was a wonder he hadn't pushed me overboard or slit my throat while I slept.

I sat in the wheelhouse during the late afternoon, smoking, coughing, drinking beer, monitoring the weather report. Fair skies were predicted. The barometer was on the rise, and, as promised, the sun began to show and the wind began to drop just before sunset. After supper I went down for a nap in anticipation of a midnight run to the Prairie.

But sleep would not come. The luminescent dial of the clock etched itself onto my retinas as the second hand lunged from post to post like a drunken sailor. I consoled myself with the fact that the clock did not tick but ran on lithium, and if I ever became too depressed I could eat the battery.

"Mike, boats are leaving. Cap'n Mike, wake up."

"Okay, okay." The clock said twelve-thirty. I was exhausted. I cursed myself for not having gotten up at eleven-thirty when I had last looked at the clock, an hour of sleep being worse than none. I lay in my bunk for a moment longer listening for the wind, but heard none, only the cough of diesels. A boat passed close astern and I struggled to my feet, strapped on the hook, and went up.

There was only a whisper of a breeze. The lights of Neah Bay played across the shore and the running lights of the trollers gave off a festive atmosphere. The sky was a brilliant beadwork of stars and lacy patches of high thin clouds.

"Only seven boats go out," Tu informed me.

"Good. We'll be out early. Weather looks great. If the fish cooperate . . ."

There was a bit of a lump left over from the storm and it had us on the beam for a time, but *Leigh Anne* paid it little mind. We left the light at Tatoosh Island in our wake. Setting our course I switched on Iron Mike, the self-steering device, and turned off the Fathometer. The radar I left on until we had cleared the shipping lanes.

Tu sat up with me for a while. I wondered if it was my imagination or if he really felt more at ease when night fell. I knew he didn't sleep long, only about four hours—I seldom got much more myself—but he seemed to wake refreshed, whereas I frequently woke exhausted. His "spot"—in the way of Don Juan— was the hatch of the fishhold. There he would squat in his skivvies late at night in all but the most inclement weather. I wondered if the world he found himself in didn't recede just a tolerable bit further in the dark, allowing visions of his own country to shine through.

After he said good-night and went below, I sat up listening to the old Jimmy chug its monotonous, reassuring song. Iron Mike clanked over and again as it adjusted the wheel back and forth. The radar showed half a dozen boats well out in front and almost as many behind. A large vessel approaching from the south would pass well to stern of us.

I drank my coffee with a shot of Seagrams, smoked my smokes, and squinted out the window trying to see the invisible: "sinkers." Submerged deadheads that could punch a hole the size of a fifty-five-gallon drum through the hull of the strongest wooden boat. They were a constant source of danger in the Northwest.

Logs, skidded or trucked to staging areas at the water's edge, were formed into booms and towed by tug to lumber mills around the Sound. Individual logs would float free, less often an entire boom would break up, and the tidal currents would spread them about the Sound, onto the beaches and out into the Strait. Once waterlogged they were inclined to assume the vertical and float just beneath the surface, rising and falling with the swells.

The world was fraught with danger, I mused; real or imagined, one could find it wherever one looked. Sea serpents could rise up out of the depths at any moment and swallow a boat whole. Or tiny little demons smaller than the point on a fish hook could spring forth from the brain-of-the-dog and drive one insane. Given a choice I'd take sea serpents any day, or night.

I struggled to stay awake, switched to black coffee. Occasionally I'd flip on the floodlight to check for sea serpents, but found none. Finally, I had to step out onto the deck before I fell asleep. It was cool. While I could feel no breeze other than the one we created, I suspected there might be a nor'easter building, which would account for the clearing skies and sudden chill. I lifted my hand to the stack and warmed it.

Dawn was coming. It would still be a time, but the sky was lightening and I could see the faint outline of the Olympics. On an impulse I stepped up onto the fish-hatch cover and tried to squat. I couldn't go flat on my heels but had to stay up on the balls of my feet. It hurt my hips and after a minute I had to stand.

I went aft to the stern and lowered myself into the trolling pit—the little foxhole in the back of the boat where I fished from. I sat looking into our wake, the wake of the *Leigh Anne*. Leigh Anne, where are you? Down in the Keys, fishing and fighting and fucking? Extremes of location: northwest to southeast. Perhaps we could meet in Omaha for dinner sometime.

Leigh Anne hadn't had much to say about Florida when she returned the previous spring, and I didn't press her. She was tan and lean. Even her titties were tan, but I didn't asked about that either. Something called to mind those ads in the boating magazines for what I call marlin boats: fancy cocktail cruisers with flying bridges on top of flying bridges, and a sweet young thing with a cork and two Band-Aids lounging on the foredeck. I imagined she'd been kept by some old Miami fart who had a boat in the Keys. Prancing the deck in her high heels and bikini bottom, while the old fart and his cronies played rummy and ogled her, she had actually been making it with the muscled young Cuban who skippered the boat.

But I hadn't wanted to know; besides, it sounded paranoid just to think, let alone say out loud. Sometimes though, when we made love, I'd make up a little fantasy about it, to keep me hard when I otherwise thought I might lose it. I had wanted to ask her to play it out for me—the high heels, panties, and the seduction—but a cold smelly fish boat didn't quite make it as a Caribbean marlin cruiser. But then neither did she own heels higher than the ones on her rubber boots.

CHAPTER 13

The opening of our third season had gone pretty much according to plan, except that there hadn't been as many fish as we had hoped for (but then I'd never known a fisherman to catch as many fish as he had hoped for). Nonetheless we did well. Leigh Anne and I tagged along with Alan and Lois, who had become a going concern. We caught our share of fish, although *Talisman* did better, which was to be expected given Alan's years of trolling. And Lois didn't seem to be too much of a hindrance, even in her thongs. I'd actually taken a liking to her, except that she encouraged Leigh Anne's potential as a chatterbox. It got to the point where I had to tell Leigh Anne to stay off the CB because she and Lois were getting to be like a couple of schoolgirls with telephones growing out the sides of their heads. She of course didn't care to be dictated to, and for a while she was not a little ticked off.

Finally, though, it took care of itself as we got out of sync with *Talisman* and started to slide down the coast. Leigh Anne didn't like it, said she liked being near Lois, but I knew I was beginning to worry her. She was watching my drinking like a hawk. Whenever we went in to unload fish and take on ice, I'd load a couple of cases of beer to take back out with us.

I wasn't getting drunk, just drinking a lot. Maintenance drinking they call it: never drunk, always drinking. I functioned flawlessly you might say, I would have said. We caught fish, I didn't slur my words, but we stopped making love, we no longer laughed together, and when the preclimactic confrontation came, I hadn't brushed her hair in weeks.

That was the real indicator of how well or poorly our marriage was going. For most couples it seemed to be sex, and to an extent it was for us too, but before the impulse to the crotch was blunted, the impulse to gentle affection was shut off. When we were happy I could spend hours just brushing her hair and nibbling on her neck. Grooming behavior the anthropologists will say, and I heartily concur.

After a particularly exhausting five days of bad weather and good fishing, during which hardly a word had passed between us, Leigh Anne stood on the dock in Westport and told me— loud enough for the fish buyer's boys to hear—that we either find the *Talisman* and start fishing with Lois and Alan or she was off the boat.

"I mean it, Michael! I've had it with your moods. If I can't be near Lois so I can have someone to talk to, you can fuckin' go fish by yourself!"

I hated having my business conducted in the open. "Leigh Anne, we'll talk about it when we're done here."

"We will not, goddamn it! We'll talk about it right now or I'm not getting back on that miserable, cold, stinking tub."

I considered telling her just why a cold, stinking fish boat was named after her, but I didn't. Instead I said, "Okay. We'll find Lois and Alan."

"Just like that?"

"You heard it."

I bought a bottle of Seagrams to go with the beer, figuring Alan would be thirsty, and we headed north along the coast. It was late in the day, and we didn't bother to fish as we went. Alan wouldn't be hard to find as there were only a couple of places *Talisman* could be. Still, I expected it would take a few days.

Finally, knowing we wouldn't catch up with them unless we motored all night, I slowed to trolling speed. We were close to shore, near an area where we had caught fish the previous year, and I wanted to give her a try before we dropped the hook for the night.

Soon after I throttled back Leigh Anne came up from below wanting to know what was going on. She looked about at the deserted coast, the absence of other boats around us. It took her a moment to realize that I was setting the gear.

"What are you doing?" she demanded.

I looked up at her face from the trolling pit, finished setting the inside port line, and moved to starboard. I assumed she knew what I was doing, and what she really wanted to know was why I wasn't pursuing Lois with all due haste. I wasn't looking for a fight. I really wanted to find a way back in with her. Back in to some warmth and closeness.

"Fishing," I said.

"I know that! I got eyes. What kind of jerk-off do you think I am?"

"I hadn't really thought about it. What kind do you want to be?"

I finished rigging the starboard lines and adjusted our course slightly with the wheel in the pit. There was a slight chop, but as yet no rain. The wind was freshening from the southwest, the first white caps showed. It was probably a waste of time, putting out the gear, but . . .

"Leigh Anne, we're here to fish. I know you'd like to see Lois so you could have someone else to talk to . . . ."

"Someone else?" she shouted. "You haven't talked to me in a week. I'd settle for anybody to talk to. Anybody other than myself. And you know what kind of a jerk-off I am? I'll tell you. I'm a perpetual jerk-off, because if I wasn't I'd never get off, and secondly I'm a complete jerk-off for coming back and thinking there was anything for me here!"

The bell on the port pole signaled company, and I started playing in the line. It came in straight and true, saying bottom fish all the way. Sure enough it was a decent size green lingcod, which some called the best meal on the end of a hook, Leigh Anne being one of them. I showed it to her with a grin, raspberries on a lima-bean green background.

She whipped the long thin blade from its sheath on the trolling cage and, without taking her angry stare from me, turned the stunned fish into a pair of handsome fillets with a couple of deft strokes. The remains went overboard.

"It's what I'd like to do to you sometimes," she said in a tone none too convincing.

"You don't have it in you."

"That's what worries me, 'cause you do." She picked up the fillets and replaced the knife. "If anything else bites your hook I'll be down below jerking off."

It had been a mistake to put out the gear. The wind rose steadily, and the stallions began to gallop across the tops of the waves. It was time to find cover. I reeled in the lines but left the poles out at their forty-five-degree angle, and dragged the stabilizers—triangular pieces of wood, one per side, that hung from the poles and bit into the water to slow the boat from flopping about. I throttled up.

We had a ways to go to shelter. Rain began to fall. There was still light in the west; it remained for a long time in late spring. In the wheelhouse I engaged Iron Mike, set a course, and went below. I could hear Leigh Anne crying in our berth.

The image of a naked back appeared in the dim light, its face hidden in hair falling about the shoulders. I undressed. It was warm with the stove going. My bare skin tingled. I stepped up behind her and ran the arc of the hook along her spine. She shivered, came up off her heels. She had on only her panties, her hands were lost before her in the dark. With the hook I swept her hair from her shoulders and lowered my lips to the soft fuzz that covered the back of her neck. I reached beneath her arm and across her chest and cradled a breast. Leigh Anne pressed her head back against mine and turning her face to me brought her fingers to my lips. Her sex was on them and on my lips and tongue. I spun her around. Sucking on her sweet taste, pulled her forward to the edge of the berth. With her free hand she found my cock, rubbed her palm to its base, and fondled my balls. I sucked harder at her fingers as she began firmly and purposefully to stroke me.

There was not enough standing head room so close in under the bow, and I was forced to press my shoulders up against the roof to maintain my balance. I pulled her up into a kneeling position, set my tongue deep in her mouth and bit at her lips. I slid the hook up under the edge of her panties, first one side and then the other, back and forth until the crotch was well up in her crack and I could gather both sides with the hook in the small of her back. She sucked my tongue and pumped at my cock as I rubbed the fabric of her panties back and forth across her pussy.

"Fuck me," she pleaded, slipping off my tongue, trying to bend her face to my crotch.

"Why should I fuck you?"

"'Cause I've been bad."

"If you've been bad, maybe I shouldn't fuck you."

"If that's how you feel about it,"she said flippantly, and let loose of me.

I yanked her panties with the hook, bringing her back to me and her hand where it belonged. "Bitch."

She laughed and squirmed as I tightened my grip on her panties. "Yes, but I'm your bitch. Fuck me. Please, pretty please." She rubbed me faster. "Please put this big thing in me."

I knocked her hand away and pushed her back on the berth. Then the boat pitched and I fell against the hull. The prop came briefly out of the water and the engine whined. I hurtled up the companionway into the wheelhouse, but it had only been a single steep face that had passed into the twilight. The coast remained a mile or so off our starboard beam with no other boats in sight. I went below.

"Where were we?"

"The last thing I said was, 'Fuck me big boy,' and the earth moved. Only you weren't touching me when it happened," she added sarcastically.

"Fingering your clit again, were you?"

"Well, if you're not going to."

"I had to save us from near disaster." I pulled her by the ankles down to the foot of the berth.

"From a fate worse than death?"

"This will be a fate worse than death," I replied, brushing the inside of her thighs with the back of the hook.

"Don't."

"Don't move." Her legs spread, her heels came up to rest on the edge of the bed as I continued to stroke her thighs with the hook. "Keep rubbing your clit." Without using the point I pressed harder, pushed closer to the juncture.

"Don't touch me with that dirty thing."

"You mean the hook or my cock?" I knelt on the floor, my face up near her crotch, my hand up on her breast rolling her nipple between my fingers. "Keep rubbing your clit."

I could hear her breath catch and feel her hips begin to move as I slipped the point of the hook up inside the crotch of her panties. "Don't stop!" I commanded. With one swift yank her panties came off. I put my face between her thighs and pressed my tongue to her vagina. She held firmly to the back of my head, and when I moved to nibble on her clit I pressed the hook to her breast. She held it firmly there, moaning and writhing as my tongue and lips brought her swiftly to climax. Her breath caught time and again, her hips came up, and her thighs squeezed my head trying to hold it back as I sought to nibble further on her.

"Enough, enough," she screamed with laughter. "I give. I give."

I let her go and dashed up to the wheelhouse to check our course. The Rock had come into sight. We would anchor in its lee; us and no telling how many others. The wind was stiff, the sea slightly chaotic, and the rain beat down on the deck. It would be good to be at safe anchor.

I sat up on the stool letting my penis droop down over the edge and pulled a pack of smokes down from the chart rack.

Leigh Anne came up after a time dressed in our threadbare wool bathrobe. She looked snug and smug. I thought I saw her glance at my equally old and beat-up meat hanging over the edge of the stool, but if so she didn't recognize it. My balls ached and I wanted to get off, but then I didn't really care. I laid the hook over one of the spokes of the wheel and smoked with my free hand. The windshield wiper beat back and forth to no avail.

She came up next to me. Straddling my leg she pressed her face to my neck and her hand found my balls. She rolled them gently in her palm and once more I began to harden. Her tongue swept about my ear, describing its curves and ridges, probing for the drum. Now, fully upright, she stroked me with long, slow movements, the flat of her thumb moving along the ridge.

We had a steadily building, following sea as we turned in toward the coast. The helm required concentration as we approached the Rock. With one eye to the depth-sounder, one to radar, and a third to the dim, darkening view through the rain-splattered window, I was having trouble concentrating on the situation in hand.

We were almost abeam of the Rock, a flat-topped, jutting island about the size of a football field with sheer walls forty feet high. The waves broke hard against its base, sending foam and spray almost to the grassy lip high above. Cresting waves broke white. Leigh Anne bent her face to my groin. With an arm around my waist, and the other moving up and down, she nibbled at the head.

I butted my cigarette and laid my arm across her back to support her as we lolled in the trough before being shot ahead on the next swell. Suddenly I laughed out loud at the incongruity of the situation: naked in the wheelhouse, except for my baseball cap and hook, and Leigh Anne bobbing at my crotch.

"What is it?" she asked, looking up at me with saucer eyes from her task.

"Nasty little blow outside and in." I laughed.

"I'm not nasty," she said, standing to kiss me, still stroking, her tongue forcing itself deep inside my mouth. "Naughty, maybe, but not nasty." She smiled and bent once more to her work.

The moment I saw *Talisman* my heart sank. Not only would I not get off, but the afternoon's intimacy would flatten and disappear like the sea in the lee of the Rock. I wanted to go on, for it not to end, but there was nowhere else for us to go. I searched my mind, but could find no way to extend the moment.

"Leigh Anne, this is *Talisman*," crackled the radio.

Leigh Anne came up out of my crotch with a shriek, dropped what she was doing, and grabbed the mike. She pressed her nose to the window. *Talisman* was the farthest out of the three boats at anchor. With her wheelhouse lit up she was easily recognizable.

"*Talisman*, this is *Leigh Anne*. Hallelujah!"

14

CHAPTER

No sooner had we tied off to *Talisman* than I began to drink in earnest. The din that Leigh Anne and Lois put up was enough to grate on the most complacent of men, and that had never been me. Even Alan, normally unflappable in the extreme, seemed put out. As soon as dinner was downed—Alan and I had consumed the better part of a fifth of Seagrams and a score of beer between us—we retired to *Leigh Anne*'s wheelhouse, leaving the women to *Talisman*.

The front had moved through. The night was clear and a cold half-moon fell on a flat sea. I went below to light the stove. Something smelled odd. I glanced about. No food lay decomposing on the table, nothing smoldered in the oven, and the engine compartment smelled no worse than usual. As I was about to mount the companionway I looked back at the berth and realized I had been sniffing the lingering odor of sex.

I went to the bed and threw back the covers. Leigh Anne's panties lay balled up beneath the sheets. I held them to my face

99

with the hook and inhaled deeply. "Cunt!" I cursed. Pulling the knife from my jacked pocket I thumbed the button and the blade snapped out. With a quick stab I joined knife and panties to the hull. A rumbling deep in my throat forced itself from between my lips and filled the fo'c'sle with mean laughter. The flimsy pink cotton hung limp from the still quavering blade as I turned and gained the wheelhouse.

At some point my conversation must have become quite disjointed for I lost Alan; and when two drunks can't follow a conversation, no matter how convoluted, there is a problem that transcends inebriation. I knew, even then, that things were about to get bad, but I was powerless to stop them. As always, it started with that crawly feeling I sometimes got on my skin, as if I'd been doing acid or smoking killer weed. When the skin began to shrink and the discomfort set in, I grew cold, my muscles contracted, and the joints grated, bone on bone. Finally the stump began to throb and the hook to grow heavy.

Outside, the silhouette of the Rock loomed in the foreground: flat, slightly tilted, with pockets of trees tall and twisted in the moonlight. The night was dead still save the steady clatter of women's voices from *Talisman.*

"Jesus Christ!" I shouted.

Alan's head jerked up. "What? What's the matter?"

"What the hell could they be talking about?"

He thought for a moment, unsure of what it was I was asking. "Oh, them. They're just talkin'. Women do that."

"Nobody talks like that. It's inhuman. Nobody has that much to say."

"Easy now, Mike. They haven't seen each other in a while. They're just talkin'."

" 'Talk to me. Talk to me,' she says. 'I can't stand it when you don't talk to me. Tell me about Vietnam. We been married two years and I don't know a thing about Vietnam.' 'Ha,' I says. 'You shoulda gone yourself if you wanted to know about it.' 'But I was only twelve when you were there.' 'Twelve!' I laughed. 'There was plentya twelve-year-old whores with tiny titties and half-naked pussies. Blow you for a quarter, kill you for a nickel. What the hell do you want to know about the goddamn war for anyway? You were in Milwaukee thumbin' your rosary, waiting for your first period.' "

Alan looked at me, eyes widening as if he was trying to wake up from a deep sleep, or a bad dream.

"You ever tell Lois about bein' in the service?"

Alan blinked, shrugged.

It was then that I saw I'd lost him. I got angry, and cold. Funny combination. The madder I got the colder I got, and the colder I got the angrier it made me.

"I got to go below, I'm freezing. Bring the bottle." I went below and turned on the light, stood before the stove.

Alan followed, plopped himself down at the table. He rubbed his face in the palms of his hands. "Six months in Thailand, Mike. No big deal. It wasn't like what you went through. Leigh Anne doesn't know that part of your life. Hell, you've never even told me about Nam. She's just curious."

"Curious!" I screamed. "Just 'cause the fucking cunt's curious, she wants me to relive my nightmares!"

"Mike . . ."

"I wasn't a bad guy, was I? You knew me, Alan. We weren't bad kids, were we? Cut-ups, maybe, but not bad, not evil. So why did it have to happen the way it did? Tell me. We went to the same high school, fought in the same war."

"I wasn't there, goddamn it!"

"Yeah, but you know. You know. Don't you think about it? Don't you dream?" I clutched my head. "Why does she have to know? I'm afraid she'll destroy me if she knows everything. Doesn't that ever worry you?"

But he wasn't listening. His gaze was fixed on the bow. "What's that?"

For a moment I couldn't find what he was seeing. Then I burst out laughing. "Panties. Panties on a skewer." When I looked around Alan was gone.

I took a pull on the Seagrams and went up on deck. My head was spinning like a gyroscope with a drug problem. Alan was nowhere to be seen, but I could hear his voice interwoven with the chattering females in *Talisman*'s wheelhouse. My skin turned hot, then cold, then both at the same time. I did laps around the fishhold cover. Eight and a half steps to a lap. Twelve laps to a cigarette. Three cigarettes in succession. I tore myself from orbit and careened into the wheelhouse. After starting up the engine I went to the rail and began frantically to untie from *Talisman*. Moments later Leigh Anne and Lois were out on deck.

"Just going off a ways," I explained hastily. " 'Fraid we might drag anchor."

"Goddamn it, Michael! We won't drag anchor, it's dead calm."

"Yeah, you don't have to move," Lois piped in.

The final line I undid as quickly as my drunken dexterity would allow. I had to get away. Get away from Leigh Anne; get away without Leigh Anne. "Why don't you stay the night with them," I blurted. "Please. Stay. I'll get you in the morning."

"You know damn well they've got even less room than we do."

I rushed to the wheelhouse. I had only to up the throttle and both she and I would be safe. But at the last moment, with *Leigh Anne* beginning to pull apart from *Talisman,* she stretched a long leg and swung aboard.

I smoked a cigarette and drank another beer before I heard her enter the wheelhouse and begin to descend the companion-way with the *clomp-clomp* of horses on cobblestones. She was wearing her wooden-soled sandals, the ones that for reasons incomprehensible to me I'd always found very sexy. Her wooden-shod feet came slowly into view, the red strap against the gray of her socks, the tight leg of her jeans, the faded knee, the snug V of her crotch, the heavy cable sweater, beige with turtleneck, too bulky to show her breasts. Her face set, eyes wide, uneasy and slightly glazed.

She stopped with one foot on the floor, the other resting on the step above. One hand was on the rail, the other disappeared above her on the ceiling of the companionway. Her hair was in a loose French braid and blond strands hung at her temples. She looked vulnerable, frightened, and impossibly sexy. At that moment I was as close to having an erection as I would be all night.

Still, she didn't drop the final foot but let it rest on the bottom step as if she might slowly back right up and go as she had come. Her eyes searched my face for clues. What she saw I can only guess, but I expect it was ugly. What I was feeling was a disconnected, interconnected array of disjointed anger, love, hate, paranoia, and helplessness.

From the hesitation and fear that showed in her face I could only guess that she was reacting to the twisted alcohol-enhanced sickness seething just beneath my exterior. Or maybe it had finally broken through to the surface and the bile deep within my soul was oozing from my pores, eating away at my skin, turning me into one massive open sore.

"What's that?" Her voice was unsteady yet demanding.

With great concentration I was able to perceive that she was referring to her underwear and my knife joined unceremoniously to the hull of the boat. It was then, as she moved gingerly from the foot of the stairs, between the table nook—where I slumped—and the stove, to the berth and the object in question, that I realized she was quite as drunk as I.

She wrestled the knife from the hull and stretched the flimsy cotton, finding the damage confined to a small puncture wound in the crotch. "Subtle. Very subtle. That's one of the things I've always liked about you."

She flung them at me. I was relieved that it was her panties and not my knife that hit my chest. She lay back on the berth, legs over the edge and feet on the floor, resting on her elbows, knife in hand.

"Frederick's of Hollywood sells crotchless panties, you know. No need to do anything as creative as make your own. I'd be glad to wear them for you if that would get you off, or up." She glared at me with a twisted smile at the corner of her mouth.

I said nothing, lit another cigarette, glared back.

She suddenly kicked off her wooden shoes, stood up, and unbuttoned the fly to her jeans and wriggled out of them. She wore nothing beneath, and the dark patch of her pubic hair clung to the whiteness of her skin like a toupee. Knife in hand she came at me, grabbed her undies from my lap, and completed the job I'd started. Then she backed up to the berth and slipped them on. Once more on her elbows, she brought her socked feet up to the edge of the bed. Her pussy stared at me from between the threads of her panties.

"Do you like?" she laughed. "You should. You like kinky undies. You're the one who bought me my first teddy and taught me to dress sexy for you." The hand without the knife went to her crotch and her finger slid between her lips.

Like the pistons of a big slow-turning diesel, my temples throbbed in and out, in and out, louder and louder, until I was sure she could hear them pounding.

She found her clit and rolled it with her left hand while the right twirled the switchblade. "You gonna fuck me or not?" she hissed, her hips beginning to buck and her breath to catch.

It was deathly hot. I broke into a cold sweat. My head was spinning. For a moment, as I tried to stand, I thought I'd pass out.

Her eyes closed and a smug smile turned her lips.

I staggered toward her, but in a flash her eyes opened and the point of the knife came up to greet me. If I hadn't caught myself I'd have fallen on the blade.

"Not so fast." She sat up waving me back with the knife. "Off with your clothes. Strip!" She laughed. Her eyes turned to slits, her nostrils flared, and her lips turned down.

I recognized this person as the fabric of threads that I had slowly plucked over the past three years and woven into the image that confronted me. I slipped out of my clothes. Not since my chopper had been blown out of the sky, making me an almost certain prisoner of war, had I felt so numbed, so vulnerable, so disarmed.

She leaned back once again. Her legs were wide, her lips red and swollen.

"Eat me!" she snapped.

"Put away the knife."

A laugh erupted from her mouth. "Never! Just once we're going to be equal. After all these years of you controlling me with the hook we're going to be equal." She beckoned with the knife. "Eat me."

I moved between her legs and knelt down. She held the knife at the ready and extended the fingers of her free hand to me. I licked them one at a time till each was clean and I had tasted the sweat of her cunt. I bent closer. The odor was pungent. I put my face in, her thighs trembled. I raised my arm, bringing the hook to rest on her belly. As I did I felt the knife caress my skin where the neck joined the shoulder. I sank my teeth into her. She cried out, pressing with the point of the knife until I let up. Putting the hook under the waistband of her shredded panties I ripped off what remained. She traced the outline of my bicep with the knife. I brought the hook up dangerously close to her flower, the petals of which looked as if they were about to exfoliate.

She sat up suddenly, bringing the point of the knife low on my belly. It was then that she saw that my penis hung down toward the sea. I stood, lest there be a doubt as to my limp lack of desire. She backed quickly away into the bow.

"You didn't really think I'd get it up for you, did you?" I screamed.

She wedged herself into the bow, panic beginning to flicker across her face.

"Nowhere to go, my pretty. You're mine now." I waved the hook at her, laughter spilling from my lips.

"Please, Michael, I didn't mean anything by it. It's just a game. You know that. Now stop it. I don't want to play anymore. You're scaring me. Michael!"

"Just a game, is it? You fucking cunt! It's not a game. It's never been a game!"

"Yes. Yes it is," she pleaded. "I'm sorry you can't get hard. But it's not my fault."

"Not get hard?" I screamed. "I can get hard anytime I want. It's just that you disgust me. Bitch! Eating away at my soul like dry rot. Trying to destroy me!" I spun in a circle with my arms thrown wide and raged at the world. Then I stopped suddenly and shouted, "Come here! Come her and suck on me!"

She didn't move but cowered in wide-eyed terror, knees drawn up to her chest, knife clutched absently to her breast.

"Come here!" I bellowed.

She trembled, shook her head no. When I lunged for her the knife slid between my thumb and forefinger, laying it open almost to the wrist.

I tried to grab my bleeding hand, but found to my astonishment that I had no other hand to hold it with, only my non-kinetic fish hook. I stared at the wound and saw myself with no hands.

A haunting sucking scream erupted as my soul fled from my body. I swung the hook at Leigh Anne with all my strength. My body shuddered at the impact as the hook embedded itself deep in the overhead deck beam. For a moment my eyes fell on Leigh Anne and a hapless smile spread across my face.

And then she was gone, screaming up the companionway.

I put my hand up to the hook to free myself. Blood splattered on my face and in my mouth. It was hot and tasted of that which fueled my life and was beyond my control. The harder I pulled the deeper the hook bit into the beam. I twisted and raged, but I could not free myself.

I hung there for a minute, sucking on my wound, breathing quick and deep. Then I unfastened the buckles and straps that bound me to the hook. I blotted my bleeding hand with the stump and found the wound to be long but not deep.

At night, on the water, a whisper cracks like rifle shot. From *Leigh Anne*'s darkened wheelhouse I could hear Lois and Alan trying to sooth Leigh Anne as they brought her in over the gunnel sobbing hysterically. The lights of the other boats at anchor flickered on the water, and voices questioned the night. I heard my name.

Lois disappeared into the recesses of *Talisman,* taking Leigh Anne with her. Alan stood still, staring across the water to where I hid. And though I could only see the outline of his face, pale and muted in the cold shadow of his deck light, I knew what it looked like, what words he gave no voice to, and I felt shame. Deep, abiding shame.

CHAPTER 15

I jumped when Tu put his hand to me. I looked about in wide-eyed confusion and lowered my arms, which I had instinctively thrown over my head. I had fallen asleep in the trolling pit and woke to a staggering sight. The sun, rising just behind the Olympics, set a coronal trail of fire running along the ridge of peaks. Rising from the edge of the Pacific, the dark-forested slopes and snow-laden mountaintops were right there. Close enough to lean out and slap! The coast of Vancouver Island stretched out over the horizon to the northwest and the Pacific shore dropped south.

The mouth of the Strait opened wide, and for a moment I knew how Captain Vancouver and his men must have felt when this massive crack in the coast suddenly appeared and the long-cherished dream of a northwest passage looked to have been found.

The wind was out of the northeast and chill; my bones ached from its bite and the awkward position I had fallen into.

"I am sorry. I was dreaming."

"Yes. I know," he said quietly.

"Have you ever seen anything like this?"

"No. Never. In mountains and countryside of Vietnam I have seen sights of such beauty to make me cry. But never have I seen anything like this. I think maybe I have learned something new about America. I often wonder how it was possible for your forefathers so quickly to throw off British. The bigness of land must make them think they could do anything, that no one could rule them."

The surface tension of the sea was almost tactile, as if a greasy, gray film had spread over it during the night. It contained the gentle roll, rising and falling, expanding and shrinking with every breath. The wound from our bow healed miraculously in our receding wake. The shadow of the Olympics rolled away from us as the sun came up and broke above the peaks. The land looked to float upon the sea.

To matters closer at hand, I could only shake my head: asleep at the wheel. The gods had been on our side and no sea serpent had reached out a tentacle and dragged me down as I dozed. No deadheads punched through our hull and no drifting boats crossed our path. I flipped on the Fathometer in the trolling pit and the bottom showed to be shallowing up. We were on the edge of the Prairie.

"How about some coffee?" I extended my hand to Tu and he hauled me up.

"I have started the stove and put on the water already. You are okay, Mike?"

"Sure. Just a little behind in my sleep."

After breakfast I again stood down in the trolling pit and readied the gear. Squarely over the Prairie, a score of trollers within eyeshot were already having at it. Tu squatted on the deck and watched me as if he would only see it once and his life depended on his being able to duplicate my every move.

The trolling rig is basic to fishing: rod, reel, and line. In this case two rods: trolling poles; six reels: gurdies; and six lines: three per pole. Pole length varies between trollers, but usually corresponds to the length of the boat. In *Leigh Anne*'s case: twenty-eight feet of straight-grained Douglas fir tapering in diameter from five to three inches over its length. Hinged to the cap rail at the aft edge of the wheelhouse, the poles can be raised slightly beyond horizontal to lean against the crosstree that extends above the roof, or flopped out at forty-five degrees for fishing.

From each trolling pole hangs a series of three tag lines, evenly spaced and just long enough to extend to the trolling pit. The pit, a small thigh-deep rectangular foxhole equipped with helm, throttle, and depth-sounder, is at the very aft end of the boat. And it is here that the action happens.

Within arm's reach are the hydraulic-power gurdies—one bank per side, three reels each. The fishing lines coil around these gurdies, passing first through blocks and then through the clips on the ends of the tag lines. As they are lowered, with a cannonball weight on the end of each, monofilament lines—spreads—are attached at approximately ten- to fifteen-foot intervals. The spreads trail a flasher and a lure: a colored spoon or a hootchie.

As each of the fishing lines is played out, the spreads are attached one at a time; the number per line depends on the depth of the bottom, but usually there are at least ten and frequently more. When the final, shallowest, spread is attached, a stopper is fastened on to the line between the gurdy and the clip on the end of the tag line. This allows the tag lines and the trolling poles to take up all the weight of the fishing lines, and all that hangs from them.

Usually it took me thirty to forty minutes to set all six lines from the outside in. Slower than most, but not bad for a guy with one arm. Afterward there was nothing to do but sit back, enjoy the sun, and wait for the fish to jump on your hooks. When the lines were full they were cleaned and reset. When the hold was full you ran into port, sold your fish, and went back out. When you'd done that enough times you tied up your boat at the dock for the winter and went to Hawaii. Nothing to it.

An hour later we were yet to land our first fish and Hawaii looked a long ways off.

We were at trolling speed, about two knots, working grids calculated with the Loran. I stood in the pit, leaning against the edge with a foot up, smoking cigarettes, eye to the Fathometer.

A sudden rise in the sea floor could take a day's, or days', worth of profits in an instant: a sixty-pound cannonball alone could cost upward of forty dollars.

Fishing—especially trolling—is a ridiculous way to make a living. With the cost of boat maintenance—not to mention payments—skyrocketing fuel bills, lost gear, fewer and fewer fish available, fewer days on which to catch them, and lower prices for those caught, it was near impossible to make a profit. Break even maybe, but little more. Still, there was nothing I'd rather be doing, and certainly nowhere else I'd rather be doing it. Especially on a morning like this.

Tu, squatting on the hatch cover, looked over at me. "Some kinda fun, Mike."

His face showed no trace of sarcasm, and again I wondered if his humor was exceedingly subtle or in translation just seemed so. "Wha'd you expect?"

He smiled. "I caught more fish when boy with my uncle."

"Wha'd you use, hand grenades?"

He laughed, but soon his smile drifted away and his expression turned melancholy.

"What is it? What are you thinking about?"

He returned from his short but distant journey and turned his gaze on me. "What life might have been, if there had been no war. Do you ever think of this?"

I nodded. "Too much, but it had to be."

"Yes. It was will of heaven. But for a moment at the end of World War Two the will of heaven almost said something different."

"Like what?"

"When war end and Japan surrender, Uncle Ho . . ."

"*Uncle* Ho? You really called him that? I thought that was just something hippies made up."

He laughed. "Oh, no. He encourage us to call him so."

"You knew Ho? Personally?"

"No, no. But once I see him. When I was very young, and served as a courier, I was in his presence . . . and he . . ." Tu, his gaze somewhere over the horizon, patted himself absently on the head.

Suddenly the bells on the ends of the trolling poles jingled, and my eyes shot to the Fathometer. The bottom had shallowed up and we were dragging. I jammed the throttle forward and this time we didn't lose any gear. I shortened the inside lines—these hung the deepest—by one spread and dropped us back to trolling speed.

Leigh Anne chugged slowly along. The outside speaker squawked CB radio traffic. Squelch, static, and "Roger that, good buddy" was an awful thing to have to listen to, but it had to be in case someone ran into trouble and needed help. I was also hoping to hear something out of Alan, who had wintered over in Westport with Lois. I hadn't seen him since he'd come to visit me in the loony bin.

Even though the season had just begun, there were already disgruntled voices on the airwaves. Didn't sound like anyone else was doing any better than Tu and I, but you never knew. Those who complained the loudest were sometimes those catching the most fish.

The bell on the port pole suddenly began to play our song. I had Tu push the handle on the middle port gurdy. As the line came up, each one of the spreads had to be stripped—removed—until the one that held the fish was topmost. As was too often the case it was the last spread, and it held not a salmon but a rock cod. It wasn't money in the bank, but it was dinner. We got it on board and reset the line.

There were four other boats working in our area. The frustration of not catching fish became more evident with each passing CB transmission. And it wasn't a ruse; too many people had too much time on their hands to be catching any fish.

Finally we hooked a salmon. The bell on the starboard pole gave a jingle and I reached out and hit the gurdy. Tu stripped the line as it came in. It was on the fifth spread down on the outside line; a feisty spring coho that shot a gleam of silver through the clear green sea.

Tu was all over me trying to see. "Big fish, Mike. Very big."

It wasn't in size, but like the inverse of never letting the first thing go wrong, you had to catch your first fish before you caught your second. So Tu was right, it was a very big fish.

I pulled it in, laid it out against the ruler etched on the deck—it was just legal—and wacked it a sharp one over the head.

Then I showed Tu how to gut it and had him ice it down. We were on our way.

The lure it had hit on was a red spoon, so I went one spread deeper and changed it from blue to red and changed the one above it also. The rest I left as they'd been: blue, white, silver. Then we pulled the other lines and changed all the spoons at the depth we'd hit to red. Next one we caught was on a blue, but it was deep, about twenty fathoms, so we bracketed the twenty-fathom spreads with blue spoons.

Like shooting skeet blindfolded, the fisherman gropes in the dark, trying to see the unseen. He changes lures, depth, direction, continually trying to outsmart the brain-of-the-dog, even if it belongs to a fish.

Tu was excited, the chase was on, and he was learning fast. He had the hunter's instinct and would make a good fisherman.

Two hours later we still had one cod and two salmon. Even the majesty of the day had begun to wear thin. There were those who swore that fish never hit when a nor'easter had set in, but an equal number swore it was the best time to fish. Some preferred a westerly, while still others liked a sou'easter. Some caught more fish on Monday, Wednesday, and Friday, while others claimed Tuesday, Thursday, and Saturday were best. What it all boiled down to was that nobody knew nothin' about nothin', except those few who caught fish regardless of the weather, the day of the week, or, I suspected, the gear they used.

I heard the bullet whisper its supersonic oath long before I heard the rifle crack. Tu and I went down in the pit compelled by the brain-of-the-dog. Knee to knee, our heads barely beneath the edge of our wooden foxhole, we stared with disbelief into each other's face. Breath held, blood surging, stomachs twisting, palms wet, instant recall.

I let out my breath. Down boy, down. I grinned at Tu. He didn't grin back, but looked quite worried.

"What was that?" someone asked over the CB.

"Shark," came the reply.

I saw Pete McGuire's face come out of the loudspeaker. I raised my head and looked to the south. There were three boats within view, and one of them was *Westerly*. It was an old East

Coast schooner McGuire had converted to a troller, and the masts had been left standing. The main held a steadying sail, and the mizzen held the rig for the poles. It was the only boat of its kind in the fleet. There was no question about it, McGuire was on the warpath.

CHAPTER 16

We ended the day with a handful of salmon and one cod; not what I would call an excellent opening, but I'd had worse. The sunset was spectacular, turning the Olympics a fiery pink, setting a fluorescent dapple of yellow-blue and red in a dance across the water to paint the backs of my eyes and leaving it there to melt away long after the sky was dark.

Tu diced up the cod and fried it along with some rice. I would have fixed it differently, but it was nonetheless quite tasty. I was becoming accustomed to an increase of rice and fried food in my diet. We ate for a time without speaking, enjoying the first silence of the day with the engine and the CB shut down.

"Mike, there will be trouble?" Tu sounded pensive, more so than I had seen him.

I shook my head. "Not that getting shot at isn't trouble, but it's just harassment."

"It is not good to be shooted at."

"Shot at."

"Yes. I have been at war all my life. I no longer wish to be fighting. For what? To catch fish? Or just because I am Vietnamese? Because I am not white? Why do these men do these things? Shoot at me. Burn your boat. Chase me from dock. I am still a boat person. I am a man with no country, like Palestinian."

He was silent for a moment then asked me a startling question. "Mike, what will happen if they come for me? Will you give me away?"

"What? Are you crazy? They're not going to come for you. Whatever happens will happen to both of us. I'd never give you to them." He nodded, but I could see that he wasn't convinced. "Is that what's bugging you? What do you imagine will happen? You think they'll come for you, all the boats in the fleet, and surround us. I'll have to give you over or they'll sink us? You've been watching too much TV."

"I think not. Everyone in America carries gun. Everything decided by violence."

"What about in your country? Vietnam has been at war for thirty, forty years."

"It is not same. That was war. A war of liberation."

"Bullshit! War is no excuse for killing women and children."

Tu suddenly slapped the table with the palm of his hand. "If you please to speak of women and children we talk of air raids against my country, when B-52 bomb hospital and school. My nephew killed in this way. By your country. At Christmas. By your Christian President Nixon and the jackal Kissinger . . ."

He stopped abruptly and I realized what an incredibly tight rein he must keep on his emotions. What a truly devastating experience it must have been to have fought all his life only to be thrown to the lions once the dream was realized.

"American people seem afraid to me, Mike. Why I do not know, but there is fear in your hearts. The white man rules America and is afraid of losing power. Losing his power to woman, black man, Indian, Socialist. Sometimes I think my country . . . Vietnam will better survive changes in the world than will America. Roots of Vietnam are very old, go back many, many centuries, very much tradition. Still, Vietnam is a new country, young and vital. People believe that they can make a new life.''

"Don't feed me that horseshit propaganda! Vietnam is a racist country just as much as America. Why the hell did they throw you out? Chinese, that's why. And the Cambodians, killing them as if they were locusts, because they're not Vietnamese. Vietnam has been at war for so long it doesn't know how to stop. It'll turn into a police state just like every other Communist country in the world.''

"So you think maybe you lose arm fighting for democracy?'' He said this with all the spite he could muster.

"Hell no! I lost my arm in defense of antediluvian American politics. What the United States did in Vietnam was an atrocity. I'm sorry I went and I'm sorry we lost.'' There it was, another of those innumerable little conflicts between the brain-of-the-dog and higher consciousness.

We stared angrily at each other. The corners of his mouth turned down sharply. He studied me with absolute contempt, and for a moment I thought he might reach across the table and rip out my throat. But at the last second he thought better of it, turned to the stove, and poured the water from the kettle into the dish bucket and took the lot up on deck.

Once during the night, when I got up to pee, I found him squatting on the fish hatch. Despite the chilling cold a nor'easter brings, Tu was clad only in his off-duty uniform of underclothes. It was a spectacular night, with no moon and more stars in the heavens than I thought possible. I stayed up on deck to have a smoke, but Tu and I didn't acknowledge each other.

The following day and the day after that were duplicates of the first: spectacular sunrises and sunsets. In between the skies were clear, the sea virtually flat, and the fishing little better.

And each afternoon we took a warning shot.

Tu inhaled everything I could tell him about fishing. He asked countless questions about the gear: When do you use this? When do you use that? Why? Why? Why?

The answer to most of these questions was "Try it.'' If it worked you were doing the right thing, and don't fix it; if it didn't work you weren't, better try something else. It was not an approach Tu appreciated—ambiguity, that is. I'd come to see that he liked things straightforward: When the situation was such and such you did such and such because.

Maybe that was the essence of the American way, for better or worse. There was no grand plan, no ideology, no guiding philosophy, other than individual fulfillment. Too often this led to: Take what you can while you can, 'cause if you don't someone else will.

But here in the northwest corner of the continental United States, room and time were running out. The Boldt decision—giving half the salmon catch to the Indians—was a statement of limitation as surely as Vietnam had been, a statement of the finite nature of America's resources as surely as Vietnam had been of our power. The American people's unwillingness to accept this made it no less true. The American way of life—the big country, the big power, and the big resources—had hit the wall. It didn't mean we were down and out, just that it was going to be a different sort of game from now on. Perhaps it would be a better one, but we wouldn't find that out until we accepted that the world, and our place in it, had changed.

CHAPTER 17

As the weather deteriorated the fishing improved. The wind shifted around to the southwest and the clouds rolled in as the barometer headed down and the high pressure broke up. The ocean turned dark but remained essentially flat until evening, when a swell began to run with the rising wind.

We started taking salmon almost as soon as the wind shifted—lending credence to one theory or another—and ended the day with thirty-six. It was one of the better days I'd had. Tu and I were both exalted. I pulled while he cleaned and iced. So excited were we that we forgot about the warning shot and were reminded only when it sounded. We started for the deck but caught ourselves up. With a quick glance at *Westerly* on the horizon, and then at each other, we went about our business as if nothing had happened.

The weather report called for sou'westerly winds at ten to fifteen knots throughout the night with a front moving in late the next afternoon. I didn't want to be chased back to port by the weather just as the salmon were making a show. We had fuel and water for a couple more days and I thought we could stick it out.

There was no sunrise the following day, save the sky turning from black to gray. At noon the gray was a lighter shade than it had been at dawn, and by late afternoon it was darkening again and went steadily that way until it was once more black. In between we landed forty-seven salmon. The CB told of the success of others, and the fact that we were not shot at I took to be as much an indication of a lack of boredom as a lack of visibility.

An unexpected thing happened that day: My guts began to ache. By midday I could barely stand the pain and had to go below. I gave Tu explicit instructions and went down for what I thought would be a short rest. I woke two hours later.

I climbed the companionway expecting to find Tu washed overboard, the poles busted, and the gear dismantled. But it was not so. Tu looked to have gotten on just fine without me. I stood in the shadow of the wheelhouse and peered out at him.

Standing down in the trolling pit, a cigarette dangling from the corner of his mouth, three good-size cohos on the deck beside him, he casually set the last couple of spreads on the line he had apparently just cleaned. He flicked his cigarette overboard—I'd finally gotten him to stop field-stripping them—pulled the gutting knife from its sheath, and deftly laid out all three fish.

"Looks like you don't have much need for me around here," I said, emerging from the wheelhouse.

"Mike, look, we do very well." He started to step up out of the pit.

"Stay put. I'll take care of these." I moved the fish to the edge of the open fish hatch and lowered myself in. One at a time I took the salmon below, chipped up some ice, and packed the pink open cavity where their innards had been. Then I stacked them like cordwood beside their cousins in a growing pile. Tu had done quite well for himself.

"How many you get?" I asked, climbing out of the hold. "Seven or eight?"

"Nine. There are many fish, Mike. Bell ring I pull in line.

Before I get fish off and put line back there is fish on other line.'' As if to confirm what he said, the bells on both poles started to jingle.

I laughed and eased myself down into the pit beside him. I hit the lever of the inside starboard gurdy. Slowly the line started in, and I began stripping spreads. Tu worked the port side. On the last spread on the deep line I found a hefty flounder. Tu had another salmon. He shrugged good-naturedly while I wrestled with the flounder. Finally, he had to help me get the thing aboard. Flounder are harder to kill than body lice, and we had to fillet the damn thing before it stopped kicking.

I hit the rack early and slept through the night. I woke feeling somewhat better, but by midmorning my guts were in an uproar. A front was definitely moving in, and so, with twenty-two fish for the morning, I decided to call it a day. We pulled the gear and headed in.

I had a chill on. I sat up in the wheelhouse wearing almost every piece of clothing I had short of my foul-weather gear. It would be a long drive home, but we had a following sea and the wind was with us. When Tu came up from below with a mug of hot soup for me, I let him take the helm and sat myself in the corner seat by the companionway.

It was not a big sea, but enough of one to give him some practice driving the boat in rough weather. *Leigh Anne* rode well. Her helm was responsive. I showed Tu how to play the swells, how to correct as the sea tried to round us up in the trough, how to throttle back if need be.

I slumped in the corner and slurped my soup. Before long I was asleep. I dreamed I was sitting in a stadium teeming with tens of thousands of people in traditional Vietnamese dress. Overhead helicopters, tethered like kites, swayed erratically, straining at the cables that held them, their engines whining, props spinning, as they twisted and dove trying to avoid each other and the rockets that were being fired at them from the crowd. Spectators stood at will. Putting rocket launchers to their shoulders, they fired up at the hapless birds. With each shot the crowd roared. Beside me a peasant woman in a conical straw hat nursed an infant with the face of an old man. The child began to cry and the woman began to scream at me. The entire stadium turned to stare: children, every one of them. Each was missing an eye or ear or nose. Their skin was burned, twisted, ripped away. Those with arms pointed, and those with tongues screamed my name.

"Cap'n Mike. Cap'n Mike! Wake up."

I struggled to regain the waking world. I pulled myself up, eyes still unfocused. The wheelhouse was dark, save the faint red glow of the compass. The wind had continued to build. Ahead, in the distance, was a light. It took me a moment to realize that it was Tatoosh.

"We're almost in," I said in amazement.

"Mike, something out there. Big boat maybe."

Listening I heard nothing but the chug of the diesel and the sea surging beneath us. Peering out the window I could see nothing but the red glow of the compass spotting before my eyes. When I put my hand and hook up to shield my eyes I felt something. Pressed against the glass the hook buzzed, and not from the tireless thumping of the Jimmy. I turned quickly, switching on the radar, the running lights, and the Fathometer.

It took a nervous moment for the radar screen to glow, and when it did I was in the midst of another bad dream. There, in the inner circle, perilously close to a direct hit on *Leigh Anne,* was a large blip. I took the wheel from Tu and turned us hard to starboard.

We flung our faces to the window. It was a large tanker, deep in the water, and going fast. They probably had us on radar, but you never knew; if they'd hit us they never would have felt so much as a shudder. It passed within a couple of hundred feet; a near miss in anyone's book. We caught its wake in deep water, and it did us no harm. The tanker showed its stern lights as it moved ahead. I put us back on course.

"When I was on boat from Vietnam to Malaysia boats like this, but very much bigger, go by. I never see such big boats in my life. I see picture of American aircraft carrier, but I think it could not be so big.

"Our boat could go no more. We have no fuel, almost no water, very little food. For two weeks we drift. Very hot. Many people die. Boats like this go by but never stop."

We passed into the Strait. The swells stacked up with every

third or fourth breaking over the stern. It was an uncomfortable final stretch that improved slightly as we passed inside of Tatoosh Island, but not until we reached the harbor could we relax.

It was always a relief to cross a bar, or turn inside a breakwater when the weather was rough, and have the sea go flat. Even *Leigh Anne* let out a sigh when we rounded Waadah Island and pulled into the harbor at Neah Bay.

The fish dock was under floodlights. Only two boats were lined up ahead of us. When our turn came we pulled under the hoist, tied off, and opened the hold.

"Looks like you boys are high boat for the day," said the fat fish buyer when I climbed up the ladder to the dock to get our cash.

"*Westerly* been in yet?"

He ran his fat finger down the list of names on his clipboard. "Pete McGuire's boat, ain't it? Not yet. Mighta stayed out."

"Mighta." I climbed back down and we moved *Leigh Anne* to the dock and rafted up beside another boat. I was tired of being fucked with, and I wasn't going to take it anymore. I refused to anchor out just to avoid another confrontation. After all, we were high boat for the day.

The weather report called for continued foul weather, so I didn't bother to set the alarm and slept until almost ten o'clock. When finally I did get up I fixed Tu and me a parcel of flapjacks. After eating I went to work on one of the gurdies that had been acting up.

Most of the fleet was riding at anchor, tucked up inside the seawall, waiting. McGuire's boat was out there, but he'd been too tired to mess with us. He'd come in during the night, and I knew it would have been a long dirty ride. I had to give him credit for doing what he said he did, which was fish, long and hard.

Tu was down below reading one of his history books, there being nothing else for him to do. He'd cleaned up after breakfast, then gone to the store and resupplied us with milk and beer. I was standing out in the rain tinkering with the hydraulics when an unexpected voice spun me around.

"Well, if it isn't the outlaw among outlaws."

"Alan!" I almost shouted, as much out of joy at seeing my old friend as relief that it wasn't McGuire. "When did you get in?"

"Late last night. It was quite a ride." He shook his head as if to say: *Don't take my understatement to be a measure of what it was really like.*

"Kicked up a bit, did it?" Like McGuire, Alan would fish as long as they were biting.

He nodded and lifted his perpetual beer bottle to his mouth. He had a beer attached to his arm as surely as I had a hook attached to mine. "That runnin' at night in bad weather . . . boy, I don't know."

Alan was the original slow-motion man. Yet he was always doing something, no matter how slowly. And in the end he always seemed to get more done than anyone else. Frequently that included catching fish. It was the same with his beer: It never seemed to go dry, remained a constant half full, and was never seen to be exchanged for a fresh. Although he was no older than me, he had the lines of an old man etched deeply into his face, and because of them had been the first one in our high school class to buy beer.

"Where is Lois?" I asked as we huddled up under the dinghy out of the rain.

"Still sleepin'. The ride in really knocked her out."

"I looked for you out there. But didn't hear you on the radio or nothin'."

"We were out there all right; down by the compass rose."

"You still workin' that old spot?"

He shrugged. "We did okay," he said in his offhanded way, which meant he probably did pretty darn good. "How 'bout you?"

"We caught a *hump.*" That stirred his interest, and I thought it might have been the first time I had a better run than him, but I'd never know for certain.

"A hundred, you say?" He lit a cigarette and thought about it for a minute. "Then this new deckhand of yours is workin' out okay?"

I nodded. "We're catching fish. And if we don't get run off the fishing grounds we might do okay."

"Heard you been havin' some trouble."

"Well, you know, with the season just opening, tensions are running a might high."

"Nothin' special?" he asked with genuine concern.

"Naw. McGuire and some of his boys. Just pushin' a little, getting rambunctious."

We looked at each other for a moment, taking the measure of what each was saying.

"I missed having you around this winter. How are things in Westport?"

"Okay. Weather even worse than Everett. Not much work, just odd jobs. Too many unemployed loggers. But Lois likes being near her family. Too near if you ask me." He shrugged.

"Give a hand with this fitting here. I'm having some trouble getting it on."

We worked on the gurdy for a bit. The rain slacked and the sky seemed to lighten and lift.

"What's the weather supposed to do?" I asked.

"Clear late this afternoon what I heard."

I reached inside my slicker for a cigarette. "We probably won't head out till morning. Sometime early if it's really going to clear. Is it supposed to hold?"

"Think so."

"Why don't you and Lois come have dinner with Tu and me tonight? Got some flounder."

Alan looked strangely uncomfortable. "I'd like to, Mike . . ."

"Tu's a great guy, Alan, really. He was a North Vietnamese Army officer. Yeah, no shit. Thirty years with the NVA. He fought against the French when he was a kid. His family was wiped out. He spent his life in the jungle fighting and then suddenly the war was over and they put him in a boat and pushed him away from shore 'cause he's part Chinese. It's an incredible story. At sea for months on a little boat with hundreds of other refugees. Attacked by pirates, out of food, no fuel, supertankers whizzing past without stopping. Year and a half in a refugee camp in Malaysia. The guy quotes American history to me. He's amazing. You'll really like him."

Alan fumbled with his beer bottle. "Look, Mike, if it were just me I'd be glad to, but it's Lois. She . . ."

"She'd like him too, once she met him. Really." I could feel my voice rising. I was about to be further cut off, and I didn't think I could take it.

"It isn't Tu, Mike. It's what happened last year, with you and Leigh Anne. Lois will get over it, Mike. You know, she and Leigh Anne were pretty tight."

"Tight? For Christ's sake," I shouted, "what do you think Leigh Anne and me were?" I turned away from him and went into the wheelhouse, closing the door behind me.

I hung up my slicker and switched on the radio. Even inside the wheelhouse I could hear the chorus the wind played in the rigging of the boats that filled the harbor. Sure enough, the weather report called for partial clearing by late afternoon, a drop in the wind, and steadily improving conditions for the next couple of days. If we left right then, we'd be on the Prairie by dark or a little later. If we left at midnight, we'd be there well after dawn, and the ride out might not be so bad, but it would be dark all the way. The current table showed that the tide would soon be slack, followed by a strong ebb. The wind had backed to the west, probably southwest offshore. And once the ebb began to run contrary to the wind, the Strait would really be sloppy. But the bottom line was that I wanted out, away from everyone and everything, and I didn't much give a shit what the conditions were.

"Tu! Get up here. We're pulling out." I started the engine.

Tu's head showed in the companionway. "We go now?"

"Now. Take the helm while I cast us off."

I went out on deck and untied us, threw the uncoiled lines down, and ducked back into the wheelhouse.

"Okay. I got it." Taking the helm I spun the wheel, increased the throttle, and pointed us toward the mouth of the harbor. We cruised slowly between boats lying at anchor, rafted up in twos and threes, *Westerly* among them. I let it be known that *Leigh Anne* would be first out, long since fishing when the others arrived.

CHAPTER 18

The outer coast of Vancouver Island runs northwest to southeast, with its southern edge turning a bit more easterly to parallel the north coast of the Olympic Peninsula, and acts as an enormous funnel for the swells that roll in across the North Pacific. Had I given a rat's ass whether we went straight to Davy Jones's locker or not I'd have turned *Leigh Anne* around as soon as we rounded Waadah Point, but I didn't. Squeezed between the narrow confines that formed the Strait of Juan de Fuca, the sea stood tall and steep.

I gave the helm over to Tu and pulled on my foul-weather gear. After instructing him to keep our bow into the waves I slid the door open, slipped my arm into the handrail bolted to the outer wall, and threw the door closed behind me. The wind whipped across the water, slicing the tops from the waves, and the deck heaved like one of those mechanical bulls so popular among folks who thought life could be experienced for a quarter. *Leigh Anne* shuddered as one wave after another tried to stand

127

her on her tail before knocking her down. But each time she rolled with the instincts of an old fighter, sliding into the trough to face the next blow with her chin down.

The sea broke across the bow, foamed along the gunnels, swirled about my ankles. For one long moment I thought of yielding, giving in, allowing myself to be sucked down the drain.

Not even Paddy—my boat-building friend—and his wife, Sue, had been close to Leigh Anne and me in the way that Alan and Lois had. As a couple, they had been our only true friends. And even though I'd never been really comfortable with Lois, or she with me, she remained a vital link between the grinding present and a past that, selectively at least, I remembered as the happiest in my adult life. Lois and I had always been suspicious of each other. She had never fully trusted me, had always felt that I hadn't been good for Leigh Anne. And time would seem to have borne her out. For my part, I thought she had tried to set Leigh Anne against me, that she had only tolerated me because I was Alan's friend and Leigh Anne's husband. Still, I couldn't deny that I wanted her to like me, and that I had been jealous of the ease of her friendship with Leigh Anne, which had seldom included me.

She and Leigh Anne may have been "tight," as Alan had explained it, and she was therefore unwilling to forgive me for what happened, but it was nothing compared with my own anguish and inability to forgive myself.

The brain-of-the-dog, still with a few teeth in his old gray head, growled low and mean. And the cowardly face of despair retreated beneath its rock. Reaching for the haul-up line I lowered the trolling poles and our wild flopping about slowed as the stabilizers dug in.

Once clear of Cape Flattery it would be better, or so I thought. What it turned out to be was different, but hardly better. No longer channeled by land, the sea was a jumble of contrary impulses. The sou'easter had blown itself out, but the swells it had created hours before roamed free, colliding with the swells the sou'wester was building. We went pitching and rolling and yawing, up and back, side to side. Green water continued to break across the bow, although not so heavily or consistently as it had inside the Strait.

Now and again I turned to Tu, who had wedged himself into the corner, and grinned at him. But he didn't seem to find the situation the least bit amusing. He sat tight-lipped and white-knuckled, cursing himself for ever having fallen in with me: another jungle fighter lost at sea.

By sundown, patches of clear sky began to show in the west. Each time we came up out of the trough we could see ourselves alone in a vast and turbulent world. White stallions still danced across the sea, but they no longer trampled us underfoot. The wind continued to drop. Two or three more hours to the Prairie, I reckoned.

I gave the helm over to Iron Mike and moved around the wheelhouse stretching my legs. Tu was below making sandwiches. He was a good deckhand, but a cook he wasn't: I'd recently lost my appetite. When Leigh Anne had been around I'd turned into a porker. That woman had liked to cook almost as much as I liked to eat.

I guess the relationship hadn't been totally genital after all. I tried to tell myself over and over that we hadn't been right for each other, that it had merely been a case of the little head telling the big head what to do. But it wasn't true. I had been in love, deeply in love, with a dollop of lust on top. But it had overflowed. And like droplets of hot creosote, it had lit the dry understory, eventually burning into a firestorm. That's how it had been the night I'd almost done her in.

After Leigh Anne had gone overboard, and *Talisman*'s wheelhouse went dark, I started the engine and raised the anchor. *Leigh Anne* motored faithfully through the black of night, crossing shipping lanes unmolested, her running lights dark and only Iron Mike to show the way.

In my madness I had no idea where I was going. I may well have set a course along the silvery path the moon laid down, but any notion that I purposefully followed it are a feeble attempt to romanticize my lunacy. I had simply lost it.

When consciousness again descended, or my memory of it, I was sitting naked at the breakfast nook with dried blood splattered across my face and arms. The back of my hand was scabbed with a large dark clot, and the switchblade lay open

on the table before me. Embedded in the deck beam at the foot
of the berth was my hook with its straps and belts dangling.

Between these objects and observations I made no connection. I had no thought to the previous night's events. No thought
for my wife, or even that I had a wife. I was a blank slate
waiting to be filled in.

Suddenly an image rushed past me, that of a half-naked woman
with legs pale, almost white. She wore a sweater, and as she
disappeared up the stairs I saw that her feet were socked. I did
not see her face, did not know who she was, but her screams
filled me with a horrible sense of dread. I shut my eyes tight,
and when I opened them she rushed past me again,
still screaming, still half dressed. I jumped up and ran after her.
Up the stairs I went without a clue as to where they would
take me.

The wheelhouse was flooded with late-morning light, and as
I stepped out onto the deck I was delighted to find myself surrounded by water. Again I was without purpose; I wasn't pursuing anyone, hadn't come on deck for a reason, was without
expectation.

This was the truly remarkable thing about going mad—this
lack of expectation. For there was no point of reference.
Everything was new, fabulous, wondrous. I knew up from down,
hot from cold, knew I was on a boat, recognized the plane that
circled overhead. But I brought no associations or expecta-
tions; there was no point of departure. Water didn't make me
think of bathing or my mother. The boat didn't conjure up fishing or the *Titanic*. I was neither undressed nor naked. And as
for the burgundy-clotted scab on the back of my hand and the
blood smeared across my arms, what of it?

I walked around the deck as if it were the first time I had
seen it. The fishing gear made no impression, just an assortment of poles, wheels, and lines. I peered into the hold and
noticed that there was ice; not a lot, not a little, just ice. It
didn't conjure up fish, ice skating, or whiskey on the rocks.

It was a warm, sunny day, with no wind, and the sea was flat
and oily. Lucky for me because I'm not at all sure that I could
have responded appropriately had it been otherwise. I returned

to the wheelhouse and there, on the chart table, was a pack of cigarettes and beside it a lighter. I picked up the lighter and turned it about in my hand. It felt familiar, friendly. I flipped it open, snapped it shut. The surface was smooth, silver, worn. "Yea, though I walk through the valley of the shadow of death I shall fear no evil, for I am the baddest dude in the valley," I read without comprehension. I brought it to flame.

Somewhere deep within the brain-of-the-dog—that reflexive scratch-and-sniff of primal consciousness—an embryonic pulsation began its slow surge to consciousness, painstakingly working its way through the tortuous labyrinth of the autonomic. Crossing and recrossing, the signal was amplified repeatedly as it passed ever higher up the ladder of prefrontal consciousness.

I sat the burning lighter gently upright, and with my fingers removed a cigarette and placed it between my lips. Regrasping the lighter I brought it up to the cigarette and inhaled. I blew out the smoke and inhaled again. It tasted wonderful. I felt lightheaded, which brought a smile to my lips.

Taking the cigs and the lighter with me out on the foredeck, I sat on the roof of the fo'c'sle and smoked and smoked. All the while the sun beat down on me, and *Leigh Anne* chugged resolutely through the calm sea and an imperceptible swell.

For a time I thought of nothing, there being nothing to think of. It was like being in the womb: warm, secure, floating, drifting. Not drifting aimlessly, for that implied something was lacking when nothing was. There was no thought of going or doing. It was very Zen, madness that is, until I noticed the asymmetry of my arms. Not just that they were different, as my hand was from my foot, but that something was missing.

I ran to the wheelhouse and down the companionway. I crawled along the floor, searching beneath the stove, the nook, the berth. Suddenly she brushed past me, and I heard her go screaming up the stairs, but I turned too late to see her face. I jumped to my feet and rushed after her.

Out on deck I was greeted by the air-popping throb of helicopter blades beating down on me. Again I fell to my belly and began to crawl. It had been a hot landing zone. As we lifted out we started taking small arms and rocket fire. There was a sudden flash, a deafening explosion, and then we were falling. I felt a jolt to my arm, as if I'd been electrocuted, and the sudden deceleration as we impacted.

I crawled the length of the boat searching for my hand. Any moment I would be taken prisoner. All about me the sea began to tremble, ripples swirled kicking into little waves. The noise grew louder, the pressure squeezing me to the deck. The vortex was upon me and for my sins I would be sucked down into hell and be made to listen to the screams of women and machine-gun fire for all eternity.

As swiftly as it had come the storm abated, although the thunder lingered. I felt an odd sense of inertia, as if the world were slowing. And then the devil appeared. He was black from head to toe and his face was a horrible sight to see, as dark as the sky at midnight. I cowered before him, weeping, whimpering.

"Hey, brother, what's happening?"

I looked up in disbelief. Something was not right, for the devil spoke jive. I began to wonder if things might not be exactly as I perceived them. I noticed the belly of the helicopter hovering high above us. Then the devil stepped closer and pulled back the black rubber hood from his head to reveal a neatly trimmed Afro. He held out his hand.

"Come on, man, I won't hurt you."

He helped me up, sat me on the fishhold cover, and checked me over, looking especially close at the wound on the back of my hand.

"So, how you feelin', bro'?"

I shrugged.

"You know where you are?"

I looked about. "Sure. Don't you?"

He nodded with a slight smile and stepped into the wheel-house, fiddled with the VHF radio, and leaned back out the door. He looked up at the big white helicopter with the red sash still hovering up and away from us, and spoke into the hand mike. I couldn't hear what was being said, but I could by then make associations of steadily increasing sophistication: radio, rescue, recovery.

My black savior put up the hand mike and waved to the chopper as it dropped closer to eye level before flying off. He put *Leigh Anne* back in gear, turned us about, and increased our speed. Evidently my flight across the Pacific had been at a somewhat less than ambitious pace, for we made port—Westport—shortly before dark.

Mr. Stanislaus—as I came to know my savior—was kind and patient, never condescending. I soon became conscious of my nakedness. He dressed me, tended to the gash in my hand, and made me a couple of peanut-butter-and-jelly sandwiches. He also encouraged me to drink a lot of water, but would not allow me to have a beer. I noticed, however, that he was not so strict with himself.

"Mr. Stanislaus," I began.

"Sylvester. Call me Sylvester, or Sly."

"Sylvester Stanislaus?"

"Yeah." He laughed. "Can you beat that? Nobody in my family knows where it came from, but there it is. Me, I think it's from a little-known African tribe that intermarried with some ancient Slavic explorers. I wrote Alex Haley to see what he thought, but, you know, the dude's got it made and don't answer his mail." He laughed again. "Now, what was it you wanted to know?"

We were sitting out on the fish hatch watching the sunset.

"You been in the service long?" I murmured, somewhat startled by the sound of my own voice.

"Fourteen years next month. Only six to go, then I'm fat. I'll only be thirty-seven and drawin' good retirement pay. Already own part share of a little dive shop in Bellingham. Doin' okay. Yes, sir."

"Did you ever . . . ever have to go overseas?"

"You mean Nam, man?"

I felt my head go up and down almost uncontrollably.

"She-it, yes. That what all this is about, dude? That what happened to your arm?"

I felt the tears welling up in my eyes as my head continued to bob.

Sylvester shook his head. "Wha'd you do, try and cut off your other hand? I found that blade down below."

"No! No, I didn't do it. She, I mean . . ." I stopped, trapped. "She didn't mean to. I mean I didn't mean to. Really, it was just . . ."

"It's okay, man. It's okay."

"It was an accident," I finally got out, starting to feel desperate. It was an explanation I would never fully make to anyone's satisfaction, especially my own.

"I was in Nam," Sly said. "In '68, '69. Doin' just what I do now, flyin' rescue. Same, same. Just don't get shot at no more."

"I flew," I blurted out. I was like a little kid starved for affection and recognition. "I was a grunt for six months. Then I was a door gunner. On a slick. Till I got shot down. Took an RPG. It was a hot LZ . . ." My realities began to collide. Hadn't I been through this recently? Today? Eight years before? "It was one of the prop blades. Came off, took my hand with it. Clean. No blood." I stared into his milky brown eyes and saw the pain go through them.

We came to the bar at Westport while there was still a faint glow in the west. Sly asked me to take *Leigh Anne* across. I felt honored. Trusted. And I basked in his approval, for the bar was breaking and I did a right fine job getting us in.

"Are the police waiting for us?" I asked as we approached the dock.

"Police? Naw, man. Ambulance maybe, but no police. You ain't done anything wrong, have you?"

I shrugged, uncertain. "How'd you come to find me?"

"Just got a radio dispatch sayin' you was missin' and might need some help. That's all."

"Did you talk to Leigh Anne? Is she okay?" Once more I saw the pale naked figure dart past. "Really . . . I didn't . . . I'd never do anything . . ."

Sly looked at me closely and shook his head. "Whatever happened, man, it'll be okay. And you just got to forget about the Nam, man. It's over. Past."

"But I see things sometimes, Sly? Don't you? Things you don't understand. Things you'd like to forget but can't?"

"Maybe I'm just lucky, bro', I can forget anything."

I looked at him hard. "You ever forget you're a nigger?"

His head jerked and his eyes went to slits. He started to say something, but the words didn't come and his nostrils worked themselves into a frenzy. "Never! And if I were to forget, somebody sure to remind me!"

I held up the stump. "Every day. And if I forget, somebody sure to remind me."

We stared hard into each other's eyes, and then Sly put out his hand and I took it in mine.

CHAPTER 19

When the trolling poles flapped out and the lines ran deep and the lures flashed, the salmon were waiting.

It was the kind of day the old-timers talk about: so many fish hitting so fast that one person in the trolling pit wasn't enough. Finally I knew what it meant to find the main vein: spring coho so thick it was all we could do to drop the gear and pick it up, strip it of fish, and drop it again. Me on one side, Tu on the other.

By the time the other boats began to show, Tu and I were in a situation abhorrent to every fisherman—long line, troller, or fly—with the fish still rapaciously impaling themselves on our hooks, we had to pull the gear. There were so many fish flopping on the deck that we had to stop fishing and start cleaning and icing or what we'd caught would spoil. And what we had were enough silver bars to dazzle the Hunt brothers.

For an hour we gutted and iced. Gulls from all over the Northwest flocked to us. Screaming and fighting they descended on us in a maddening din. If the boats now working in our vicinity weren't doing every bit as well as we were, this mob of gulls would certainly alert them.

The radio had been strangely quiet, and I'd just assumed that everyone else was catching too many fish to be jabbering. But the more I thought about it the more I realized that if even a tenth of the fleet had been doing half as well as Tu and I there'd be some bloated chest letting the world know about it.

Finally we got caught up enough for me to put the lines out again, leaving Tu to finish icing the rest of the fish down in the hold. Once more the bells on the trolling poles began to jingle like the bells on the cash register. They hit everything that day, regardless of the color or the depth of the lures. They would have hit on paper clips and safety pins if we'd been dragging any.

Almost imperceptibly I noticed the other boats closing in. They weren't on top of us, and I don't mean they were "after" us, but they were behaving in the not-too-subtle manner of fishermen who suspect the other guy to be doing just a little better than they, and maybe it wouldn't hurt to just sort of slide on over and take a look.

Among them was *Westerly*. McGuire's presence, and the obviousness of the maneuver, however subtly executed, furthered my suspicion that for some unexplainable reason Tu and I were the only ones catching fish hand over fist.

It didn't make sense though. We'd caught too many fish for it to have been just a pocket, and we were still catching them. Even though I had tried to keep us in the same area, even when we had stopped to clean and pack, we had unavoidably drifted off. But that hadn't stopped the fish from hitting. I could have accidentally set the lines too hot or too cold, and they had turned out to be just what the salmon were after, but it seemed improbable. Most of these guys had been trolling longer than I had, knew all the tricks, and could catch fish if there were any to be had. Except today.

Not that I wasn't a little puffed up at the prospect of catching more fish than the rest of them, especially McGuire. He was a highliner, and not by accident.

But along with the reputation—as every gunslinger knows—is the pressure to remain the best, the fastest. And while I wasn't exactly the new kid in town, McGuire had a vested interest in outfishing me. So to see him slide down on me, as he was—and without firing a shot—I just had to figure he was doing none too well. He'd know that I knew what he was up to, and it must have galled him.

As I watched Tu, shoulder-deep in the hold, lifting the freshly gutted pink-fleshed salmon from the deck and disappearing from sight with them, I pondered his role in all this. Was he the wild card? Was Tu really my lucky charm? While I didn't believe in magic, voodoo, or organized religion, he was the only variable that came immediately and repeatedly to mind.

We had caught so many fish I was giddy. Two hundred seventeen, I counted. It would have been a big week; in a day it was staggering.

Tu and I washed the smell and the slime from ourselves the best we could, but we would stink till we made port again and could shower. Our hands bled from handling the lines and our shoulders ached for the same reason. We laughed every time we looked at each other, uproarious, cosmic tickle laughter.

The competition had backed off just before dark. I could see them out there in the outer circle on the radar, licking their wounds, waiting, conniving. Little glowing specks that came and went with the sweep of the arm. Clustered together in a loose configuration, they were far enough apart not to drift into each other in the night, but close enough to hear the echo of the sea slapping against their empty holds.

We ate spring salmon for dinner. Fillets off the tail, so red they looked like beef, and so juicy they hit your tongue running and slid to your gullet with only a gulp. I opened a bottle of good red wine that I'd stashed for just such an occasion, and we toasted our good fortune.

"You ever get around Hué?" I asked him.

"Oh, yes, many time. It was magnificent city, before you destroyed it."

"Me? I wasn't even there when it happened." I grinned.

"The Americans. Your side. However you call it."

"But you wanted us to. You made us do it by going in and staying until we leveled it, then you split. You did it for propaganda, so you could say to the world, 'See what the Americans have done? Destroyed one of the most beautiful cities in the world.' Isn't that true?"

"Well"—Tu shrugged—"I did not make those decisions."

"Just following orders?" I said sarcastically, thinking of my own role.

"No. That not what I mean. It not for me to make propaganda decision."

"So it was propaganda!"

"I think in America you believe only Communist make propaganda? Yes? Propaganda is only to persuade someone to believe a certain thing. American radio and television is full of propaganda. You call it advertisement. In Vietnam we not so cynical. We call it propaganda."

"But you do admit that Hué was destroyed for propaganda?" I insisted.

Tu sloshed his wine about in his mug, contemplating its blood-red color. "Perhaps. It was part of Tet. Beginning of end, end of beginning. America lost heart after Tet. For us it was great propaganda victory, even though we suffer terrible losses. Maybe it was worth the cost. Still, the battle for Hué was a terrible thing."

He stopped to light a cigarette. "I had no stomach for the war after Hué. I had visit Hué as boy with my father when the *cây-dai* trees are in flower. The Perfume River was great, the walls of Imperial City reach to the heavens. The city alive with people: in the parks, on the streets and the river. My father was on business. We stay with cousin of my mother's sister. I spent days walking city, outside the walls of the citadel, crossing and recrossing bridges over Perfume. Thirty years later I help to destroy all this. Piece by piece the wall fell beneath your guns and planes. Ancient capital of Aman lay in ruins as we had planned."

"You executed thousands of civilians at Hué, didn't you?"

Tu slowly nodded his head. "I was fighting for more than twenty years. I had live most of life in jungle fighting French and Americans. War was my life. I know nothing else. Many, many years of hardship, living like animals in jungle with little to eat and only faith and will of people to carry on. Our aim never changed: Vietnam for the Vietnamese." Here he laughed bitterly. "If only I had known how true this was. But our methods changed, and our spirit also.

"In early years, fighting French"—his face lit up with the memory—"it was not unusual to see Uncle Ho or General Giap or Pham Van Dong. We were strong and pure then. Full of idealism, dedicated to a free Vietnam and new socialist state. I was young, committed to the destruction of the French. I rose quickly to captain. But, as you have been so kind to demonstrate, I never become major."

Tu again fell silent and smoked his cigarette in that fashion peculiar to Vietnamese—or so it seemed, even of the youngest boy—with the cigarette held between the second and third fingers near the tips, the fingers parallel and the thumb neutral. The mouth and chin were eclipsed by the slow deliberate motion of the hand. And the smoke was inhaled slowly and expelled in clouds, drifting mists, never spurts or steaming snorts. It was a more feminized mannerism than Americans allowed for, and had a decidedly Continental or European flavor.

"After Hué destroyed and people executed I lost my heart for battle. A year later I was sent north and put in charge of training regiment. A place where young men came to prepare for fighting."

"Basic training."

He nodded. "I still believed in the revolution, and I saw that our young men were well trained. But I knew I would go no further; I was in disfavor. The war went on and eventually it became clear that we would win not only political victory but military. And with total victory there was no restraint." Tu again inhaled deeply on his cigarette and let the smoke drift away.

"Enough of this war shit," I cried. "We are fishermen."

"Yes," he smiled. "We are fishermen."

"And damn good ones. You know how many fish we caught today?"

He nodded his head vigorously. "Lots."

"Yes!" I cried. "Lots and lots." And we laughed some more.

"I do not think Cap'n McGuire caught lots, do you?" Tu asked with a devilish smile.

"No! I do not think Captain McGuire caught lots of fish today."

"We make very much money?"

"Very much."

How much, how much? his eyes asked, but his voice was silent.

"Two, three thousand," I said, not wanting him to burst from struggling with propriety and curiosity.

"Dollars?" His eyes were wide with disbelief.

"Yankee dollar. Your share is two or three hundred."

"Just today?"

"Just today. But tomorrow"—I shrugged—"tomorrow maybe nothing."

He shook his head. "No, tomorrow even better."

CHAPTER 20

Damned if he wasn't right. We did catch more fish the next day, by thirty-five.

It was a long, exhausting day. The sea had a good lump to it. Pushed by a stiff wind it turned to white caps and began to break by midday. The deck, slippery with fish slime and rain, danced beneath our feet. I had a hacking cough and my guts ached. Never seasick, I'd been unable to keep breakfast down and had had the dry heaves all morning. I desperately needed to go below and rest, but the goddamn fish wouldn't stay off our hooks.

Tu and I huddled in the trolling pit, yellow hoods of our slickers up over our baseball caps, cigarettes dangling from our lips. The gulls hovered above like flies. Visibility came and went, from the tips of our trolling poles to a few miles at best. When the gray lifted we'd rise up out of the trough and there would be another boat in the distance, riding the swells, attracting but a few gulls.

Once that distant boat was McGuire's, and I could see him on the deck in his slicker with his red beard hanging down from his face like a bib and his hat pulled low. Despite my inability to see his cold blue eyes boring into me through the distance and the damp gray fog, I knew they surely were. Then the fog would lower over the gray-green sea, closing us into our own private worlds.

I had to keep close watch on the radar that day, which meant frequent trips to the wheelhouse for the trolling pit had only a Fathometer. I didn't care to have someone loom up suddenly out of the fog—accidentally or not—and foul our gear. It wouldn't take much to bring the whole works crashing down.

Tu was a dynamo. He was nimble, didn't seem to notice the pitch and roll of the boat, had never so much as mentioned seasickness, and had an uncanny ability to conceptualize. Rarely did I have to show him more than once how something worked before he mastered it. He had understood immediately the trolling rig and what went on out of sight beneath the surface. The electronics—Fathometer and radar—he instantly grasped, and I had been tempted to inquire if he had commanded an antiaircraft battery at some point in his career, but thought better of it. He seemed able to block out all but that which applied to the task at hand. He would have been a formidable soldier.

For a time we both pulled fish. When the pile began to mount I had Tu start cleaning. He could clean faster than I could pull, and the pile on the deck dwindled while the hold slowly filled.

After a while we switched off, but he was still faster—could clean the lines and reset them faster than I could gut and ice—and in no time the pile on the deck was growing again. The chill had a hold of me that day. The rain continued its steady, gentle descent, and I sweated miserably inside my foul-weather gear. The day being what it was, the fish would not quickly spoil, and I pulled myself once more from the hold and went below to see if I could get something in my stomach.

I cranked up the stove, put on a can of soup and the leftover coffee from breakfast. I slumped in the nook and promptly fell asleep. When my head slapped against the hull I woke to find the soup burned and the coffee boiling away. After fixing a sandwich I went up on deck and sent Tu below.

It is usually impossible to look at a salmon without seeing a price tag on it, but that afternoon I might as well have been shoveling coal as stacking silver. I knew we were doing great, catching a gaggle of fish, making a hoard of money, but it was an incredible effort to move about. In my damp clothes and cumbersome foul-weather gear I felt like the Tin Man before Dorothy happened along. I knelt on the heaving deck oblivious to the chug of the engine, the cry of the gulls, and, fatally, the approach of enemy boats.

The fish slowed their suicidal impulses long enough for me to gut a few of the scores still scattered about the deck. I slid the gutted fish to the edge of the hold and slowly lowered myself in. One at a time I brought the fish below. I chipped ice and packed their hollow cavities. I added them to the stacks in the port bins, careful to keep the load evenly distributed throughout the hold, and finally packed the top row with more ice.

I pulled myself to my feet, and as I stood I was confronted with the unexpected and unreal sight of boats to either side of the *Leigh Anne*. To starboard was *Westerly* and through the window of the wheelhouse I could see McGuire looking for all the world like the devil himself. Framed in glass, peering out with mad determination, he pulled his boat close alongside. His dim-witted deckhand stood on the heaving deck about to throw a line around my starboard trolling pole. To port the drama was repeating itself. This boat was the *Miss Mary*, another Everett troller. I didn't know the skipper, but I'd seen him about: a sallow-complected Johnny-come-lately with a clipped moustache that made him look like a refugee from the British Indian Army.

They worked it out in nifty fashion actually. Their trolling poles were straight up—mine were of course out—so they could lay off me without colliding. *Leigh Anne* was still puttering along at trolling speed. As *Miss Mary* went up on a crest, *Leigh Anne* went down in the trough, making it no more difficult to get a line around the trolling poles than to hang your hat on a rack. Then *Westerly* went up on the other side of me and McGuire's deckhand lassoed the other pole. They had me good and proper.

All I could do was stand chin-deep in the fishhold and watch, mesmerized by what was happening. Had I the strength or the presence of mind to scramble out of the hold, I might have gotten to the rifle in the wheelhouse and forced them off. But I had neither.

When the poles finally did go, as *Westerly* and *Miss Mary* pulled away, it was with a terrible crack. The rigging came down, and the poles flopped about like gulls with busted wings. The port pole came down without actually breaking, but it was severed from the rigging and all but sheared off from the hinge plate where it abutted the rail. The starboard pole snapped in half and swung wildly across the deck, threatening to demolish the skiff and the gurdies.

Tu was out on deck by then, having had no idea that anything was amiss until the poles crashed down. He stood in the door of the wheelhouse and immediately assessed the situation. He gave me an arm up out of the hold. We threw on the hatch cover and went to work securing the port pole before it did any more damage.

At first I was more bewildered than angry. The sea and the fog and the gulls squealing overhead were not at all different than they had been moments before. Yet *Leigh Anne* was badly busted, and there'd be no repairing her at sea.

Once the poles were lashed down and Iron Mike set a course for Neah Bay, Tu and I each took a bank of gurdies. Slowly we reeled in the lines, untangling the spreads with their silver flashers and hooked spoons that wrapped and twisted around each other and the stainless fish lines. It was a slow, laborious task. As I worked I recalled a story I had once read entitled "A River Runs Through It." The author was an old man named Norman McLean, and it was the story of two brothers who revered fly-fishing above all else. One day the brothers were fishing *their* river—a big western river in Montana—and the younger of the two—indisputably the better fisherman—fishing across the river from his brother, was having no success while his brother was "ripping lips," pulling them in one after the other. Finally, in desperation, unable to bear the sight of his brother's success any longer, the younger brother threw a rock into the hole where they were fishing, scattering the remaining fish. The older brother, far from being angered, took this as a high compliment.

It is a memorable scene from a remarkable story, and I consoled myself with the illusion that McGuire had been throwing rocks in the river. Of course the love and humanity from "A River Runs Through It" were noticeably absent, and the price to pay—a few less trout for their dinner versus the time, money, and lost fishing these repairs would cost us—was hardly comparable.

I vowed I would hurt McGuire for this.

CHAPTER 21

When I woke I had no idea where I was. As I tried to sit up I
hit my head on the upper berth immediately and located myself. I lay back and listened. Something was not right. It took
an effort to realize that what I was hearing was what I was not
hearing: the Jimmy diesel at its steady, laborious task. And the
sea was calm. I heard the rain drum lightly on the roof and the
squeak and rub that said we were tied up to the dock. Slowly,
I swung my legs to the floor and stood. Tu's shadow lay curled
in the upper berth. I went quietly up the companionway into
the wheelhouse.

Neah Bay lay crouched beneath the low clouds of night. Many
boats were in, many were not. *Leigh Anne* would not have been,
except for the unexpected need for repairs. Flashlight in hand
I stepped out onto the deck and lifted the hatch cover. The light
dug about in the corners but found no fish. Like a thief, I returned to the wheelhouse with the probing light and pulled out
the fish register. There, penned in a foreign hand, was the entry

149

for our two days' catch. One, nine, four, four. Almost a ton of fish. I dialed in the combination to the cash box, but it held only what I had last deposited. Tu did not have the combination.

It had been a very long and uncomfortable ride in; with the poles down we had been unable to drag the stabilizers and had flopped about wildly. Still hours from port, my guts aching, I had lain down to take a nap. Obviously I had overslept. Tu had brought us in, sold our fish, and tied us up at the dock. I'd had virtually nothing to do with the biggest haul of fish I'd ever made. For my part I had merely directed us to the fishing grounds and put us into a slow circle. Almost single-handedly Tu had caught, cleaned, iced, delivered, and sold nearly two thousand pounds of spring salmon, and in the process had caused the boat to be practically dismantled.

All the while I was slipping deeper and deeper into some sort of unexplainable lethargy. I began to wonder if Tu wasn't slowly poisoning me. It sounded unbelievably paranoid. Still, I had been healthy, strong, and fit before Tu and I had started living aboard together. Now, I had no energy, no appetite, and a hacking cough. My guts ached, I was nauseated, and I couldn't stay awake.

It wasn't so farfetched, Tu wanting to poison me. Underneath his calm, *inscrutable* exterior was a deeply bitter man. He had every reason to hate America and Americans. We'd tried for twenty years to impose our will on his country, first by financing the French's attempt to do so, and then through direct intervention. We'd bombed his cities, defoliated his countryside, destroyed his culture, uprooted and killed a substantial portion of his countrymen. Couldn't say I blamed him for being more than a little pissed off. What better place to aim his hatred than at me? I was close at hand, and had been part of the effort to subjugate his land. It might not be rational, but there was really no way to comprehend fully the trauma of his life.

Maybe he imagined that if he killed me he would somehow get a hold of *Leigh Anne*. But if he just wanted the boat to escape in—where did he imagine he could get: Mexico, Canada, even Vietnam?—why not just push me overboard when we were out on the Prairie. Lord knows that would have been easy enough. But to remain above suspicion, and keep *Leigh Anne,* slow poisoning might be the answer. Did he imagine he could be his own master? Was there a friend in Seattle he would bring in for a deckhand? That's what the other fishermen kept saying: Let one in and all their goddamn relatives will be fishing before you can turn around.

Through the windows of the wheelhouse the light began to shift from black to gray as day replaced night. But the rain, the interminable rain of the Northwest coast, still fell.

I boiled coffee water while Tu slept on. Then it struck me that there could be no better way to feed me on a slow steady dose of whatever it was he was giving me than through my coffee. It was freshly ground and highly aromatic, so it would overpower the smell of any additive. Strong enough to hide most any taste. On top of which he always added more sugar than I liked! And Tu didn't drink coffee, only tea! Most diabolical of all, I could dish it out to myself, just as I was about to do.

I went up to the wheelhouse with the coffee and an old newspaper. I poured the grounds out on the flattened paper and shifted it around as if I were panning for gold. I put my nose to it and sniffed about like a bloodhound, but succeeded only in snorting up a nostrilful of Colombian brown. That I could see or smell nothing proved nothing; whatever he was lacing my coffee with had obviously been absorbed into it. The wily ways of the NVA were well known.

But it was too absurd, too paranoid, even for me. I'd virtually taken Tu in off the street. He would never hurt me; if anything he was loyal. He'd proven that through his mindless devotion to the revolution. Shit, they'd shown him where dedication to the cause would get you. He might as well have been a Moonie. Mindless collective consciousness. Do what you're told when you're told. Fight, fight, fight. Kill, kill, kill. Anything for the people. It was a way of life. He'd said as much himself. Ever since he'd been a child he'd fought the enemy. Why should he stop now? He'd probably been a Psych-Op officer in charge of torturing local village chiefs or captured U.S. pilots. That bleeding-heart bullshit about the massacre at Hué had completely hoodwinked me. There was obviously some simple substance you could get in the health-food store or one of those Chinese herbal shops in Seattle that made a wonderful tasteless, odorless poison. How fucking stupid could I be to take on a gook for a deckhand? I tossed the coffee overboard, pulled on my wool jacket, and went into town to have breakfast.

I stood outside in the rain for half an hour waiting for Captain Hake's Diner to open. I had a chill on, but it was worth the wait to get some food into me that wasn't taking any years off my life. I ate heartily and felt better for it. I decided it was probably a good idea to lay off the coffee altogether for now. It might activate whatever Tu had put into my system. A few days without coffee—maybe even booze—would be good for me, get me shipshape again. And if it didn't . . . Well, then perhaps Tu didn't have anything to do with the state of my health. I was willing to give the guy the benefit of the doubt. After all, I liked him. It pissed me off that he was poisoning me, if he was, because I considered him my closest friend. Maybe my only friend.

When I returned to the boat Tu was squatting in his typical peasant fashion on the hatch cover, wearing his flip-flops, Frisco jeans, and wool shirt, drinking tea, smoking a cigarette, and generally ignoring the heavy gray mist. "Cap'n Mike. Look, look," he exclaimed, springing up and going into the wheelhouse.

His exuberance was more than I could stand. I wanted to kill him on the spot. But I knew I'd have a tough time talking my way out of it—no matter what sort of support I might get from the fishing community—if a shot was heard and Tu was found sprawled on the deck with a slug between his eyes, and a rifle was in my hand.

I stepped aboard trying to combat the rage that festered within me. I lit a cigarette and forced myself to look at the damage done to our gear. The port trolling pole was busted at the butt where it fastened to the hinge on the rail. The pole could be shortened and the hinge straightened and refastened to the rail without much trouble. The rigging that had come down with it would not be so simple, but nothing a little time and money wouldn't fix. It was the starboard pole and rigging that were really going to be a pain in the ass. Busted a third off, it would have to be replaced, and all the rigging and hardware removed and put back on the new pole.

"Look, Mike!" Tu stepped out on deck holding an envelope stuffed with greenbacks.

I took it and ran my thumb across the wad of hundreds, fifties, and twenties. Two, three thousand easy, just like it said in the ledger. Keeping everything nice and neat, he was. Trying to keep me off guard. I handed it back to him without comment.

His exuberance fell away and his cool exterior moved up to cover his face. "Did I do wrong?"

I shook my head.

"You could not be awakened last night. I thought it best . . ."

"It's okay, Tu. You did right. Everything is fine, just fucking fine."

"The book." He pointed toward the wheelhouse and started for the ledger.

"No." I waved my hand. "I saw the book. It's okay." The guy was nervous, and I didn't want him to know I was on to him. "You did great, Tu. The book is perfect, the money is all there. You got us in. I couldn't have done it better. Put the money in the wheelhouse." I tried to smile but couldn't, and turned back to my assessment of the damage.

I smelled it before I saw it and wheeled around.

"Here is coffee for you, Mike."

All I could see was a hideous yellow face and a mug of steaming black poison extended toward me. I swung the hook, knocking the mug flying, shattering against the deck.

"You son-of-a-bitch gook bastard! What are you trying to do to me?" I screamed, advancing with the hook out.

Tu backed against the engine stack. "Do not say this thing, Cap'n Mike. You have no right. What is matter with you? Are you crazy?"

Crazy?

I lowered the hook and backed away, turned away. I stepped off the boat onto the dock and started to walk away. But after a few steps I turned around and reboarded. Kneeling on the deck I crawled about, raking in the pieces of white ceramic

strewn about. Tu helped and we had all but the smallest frag-
ments within moments. We stood, hands cupping the damage,
and glowered at one another with fear and suspicion. I tossed
my handful overboard and he did the same.

"There's a tool box down below in the engine compartment.
Bring it up and take the hardware, this stuff." I showed him on
the busted trolling pole. "Take all of it off. I'll see what I can
do about getting us another pole. Okay?"

Tu nodded.

Finding a pole and getting the rig operational once more turned
out to be a lot easier than I had imagined. I asked around the
docks after one, and in no time a fellow put me on to another
who gave me the phone number of a guy who not only had one
but offered to deliver it. When he got to the dock in his pickup
and saw my hook, he offered to help carry it down to the boat
and I didn't refuse.

"Caught too many fish, did you?" was all he said when we
got to *Leigh Anne* and saw Tu.

"Something like that," I replied, knowing he'd heard the story.
I paid him what we'd agreed upon and he went away.

We'd lost some fittings, and after looking at the general condition of the ones Tu had salvaged, I went ahead and replaced
those also. We worked in the drizzle without speaking, and when
it came time to eat I took him up to the diner and we ate in
silence.

Throughout the day fishermen wandered by—most of the fleet
was out, but there were always guys in with breakdowns, or
dropping off fish, refueling, and reicing. Most everyone knew
us by then: Captain Hook and the Alien. Besides, we were—or
had been—catching fish, and it didn't seem like many others
were. Curiosity brought most of them by, just wanting to see
who was causing such a stir. Others hoped to learn the mystery
of our success; these sidled up to us real friendly, and regardless of what direction the conversation started—and I always
let them start and lead it—it always came around to what were
we using for lures, how deep were we fishing 'em, and where.
And I told them, told them the truth, everyone who asked. Of
course they didn't believe me, because Tu and I weren't doing

anything different than they were, except we were catching fish
and they weren't.

By the end of the day Tu and I were laughing over it. Tu
even had a fair imitation of how the conversation went.

"Howdy, boys," he'd say if he was imitating an older guy,
or "How's it goin'?" if it was someone younger, followed immediately by, "Good day for it," meaning the weather. Then,
"Doin' a little maintenance, are you?" The giveaway was always, "That's what you get for catchin' so many fish." Tu had
that one down. Once they popped that one they were committed: "Whatcha using, how deep, and where?"

The exception was the guy who stopped by to tell me I was
a fucking asshole and Tu was a slanted-eyed bastard. It was a
refreshing change, but I'd been feeling mighty guilty for having
called Tu the same things. So I ran to the wheelhouse for the
rifle, but the fellow didn't wait around to see if I'd use it or not.

I'd half expected McGuire to come motoring on into the harbor, but he never did. He might have slid down the coast, but
I knew that was wishful thinking. He was probably still out on
the Prairie content that I wasn't and making the best of it. He
might have found the vein by then and was sockin' 'em, but if
it was just scratch fishing he'd be doing what good fishermen
did, and that was fish longer and harder.

That I felt rested and energetic the next day only added to
my lingering suspicion that Tu was somehow responsible for
my lethargy and the pain in my stomach. Only twenty-four hours
of not eating the food on board, including the coffee, and I was
beginning to feel my old rambunctious self. We continued to
take our meals at the diner.

How I would handle the food situation once we went back
out I hadn't figured. I couldn't very well lock it all up and not
let him have access to it. On the other hand, I couldn't go without coffee. I thought I could get by if I watched him closely
and could figure out some way to secure the coffee.

The boat was ready. The repairs had cost relatively little in
hard cash: I had a couple of spare cannonballs (we'd lost two),
extra monofilament, flashers and lures, but they'd all have to
be replaced eventually. In lost fishing it was impossible to say,

but we'd lost two days, and during the previous two we'd made close to three grand. It was unlikely that two days like that could ever be duplicated; it was a season for a lot of guys.

Tu continued to regard me cautiously and retreated into his inscrutable Oriental-deckhand role. I considered giving him the boot, but I couldn't fish alone. And even if I'd lynched him from a streetlamp in Neah Bay, it wouldn't have improved my image enough to get me another deckhand. Besides, he caught fish.

When we finished the repairs to the boat, it was, if anything, in better shape than before. The revised weather report called for the wind to build, and I decided to hang tight until a clearer pattern emerged. No point heading out to be met halfway by a front. Besides, another day in port made me another day stronger before I had to wrestle with Mr. Tu of the NVA.

CHAPTER 22

At two A.M. I rolled out of bed feeling not half bad. In the wheelhouse I switched on the radio, poked my head out the door, and sniffed the night. The harbor was still. A faint breeze ruffled the water and fingered the rigging. Small patches of stars showed through the clouds.

The weather report confirmed what my senses told me. I started up the engine then went below and did the same to the stove. I put water to boil and pulled fresh coffee from my locker, which I had secured with a padlock. Tu had seen me lock up the coffee but hadn't said a word. I guess he knew I was on to him, but there wasn't much he could do about it. Whatever it was he'd been giving me was obviously some slow-acting agent that he could only hope would catch up with me before I caught up with him. If that didn't work he'd have to put me overboard.

It would bring a lot of heat down on him, but guys were forever going over the side, even on the calmest of days. How he thought he'd end up in possession of the boat I didn't have the slightest—some demented thought process obviously—unless, as I've said, he was thinking of heading for Canada or Mexico. I'm sure he hadn't counted on my getting wise to him. All that was left was for me to spring it on him first.

Tu got up and dressed. He drank the cup of tea I'd made for him, then cast us off and pulled the bumpers on board. Slowly, I headed *Leigh Anne* for the mouth of the harbor. A dozen trollers rode at anchor, scattered about in rafts of twos and threes. Their dark squat forms showed us no interest as we passed. But one of them suddenly grabbed my attention. I spun the wheel and throttled back, putting us into a slow wide turn. *Westerly* was on one end of a raft of three, only her night lights showed faintly, high in her rigging. As we crept by, twenty feet from her stern, I put my nose to the window and peered out.

I wasn't sure what I wanted to do, if anything. But the longer I stared at *Westerly* the more infuriated I became. Son of a bitch had cost me hundreds of dollars in repairs and untold thousands in fish. And no, I wouldn't turn the other cheek.

I gave the helm over to Tu, took up the rifle, and chambered a round. I had Tu bring us about so that any shots passing through *Westerly* went on out into the Strait and not the harbor. I stepped out onto the deck and flickered off the safety. Unable to see if anyone lingered in *Westerly*'s wheelhouse, I fired the first round high. Then I brought the muzzle down and quickly squeezed off eight to ten rounds that shattered the windows and punctured the walls.

"Listen good, McGuire! You motherfucker! You come anywhere near me again and I'll cut your balls off! You hear me?"

But there was no reply. And the harbor remained asleep as though I raged in a dream.

We didn't catch squat that next day, except cold. It rained and the sea was choppy. My guts ached, and Tu was sullen. I was sure he was doing something to fuck up the fishing to get back at me 'cause I wouldn't drink his coffee.

That night it blew at least thirty. I put out the poles and the stabilizers, which helped some, but it was still your basic uncomfortable night. Tu and I hardly spoke. He put himself down early with his history books while I stayed up in the wheelhouse drinking and smoking, watching the waves.

What was it my mother had told me? Leigh Anne had a fella? Yes, something like that. Sucking on some other guy's toes, she was. Maybe it had been lust all along and not love. But how did you tell? We'd cared about each other. Been loving. Been intimate. And then there were those emotionally dangerous moments where I'd crossed the line and been unable to get back.

Maybe the problem had been that the risks we'd taken and intimacies we'd shared had only been sexual. We'd built an upside-down pyramid that had no place to go but aground. But how did one share the emotions of another world? Sure, we'd come from roughly the same culture, had had the same hopes and dreams, and a few of the same fears. But I'd gone sideways through a time warp, and unlike space travelers—for whom time slowed relative to the earthbound—I'd shot so far ahead through time and horror that I'd lapped a generation, come back among peers, having lived twice as long, having experienced things they couldn't imagine. And worse, I'd had no words to describe them with.

It wasn't the fault of those left behind that they still had the beliefs and ideals of the uninitiated; I could only envy them their ignorance. And rightfully so, for who needed to live two lives by the time they were twenty? Children had the need to grow up slowly; it was biologically inherent in the species. Still, there was something so protected about American children, even the grown-up ones, that it cemented their vision in blissful ignorance all their days. And if by some quirk of politics, poverty, or ignorance you had been wrenched from the adolescent bliss of the great double play to face a reality so different and so horrifying, there was no looking back.

The wind set up such a din, howling through the rigging, that despite my desire to be alone I was forced below deck where it was somewhat quieter.

Tu lay in his berth reading. I couldn't blame him for how he felt about me, wanting to do me in. But we'd lost the war. That was enough. I couldn't be responsible for what went on after we'd departed his country or for his country's racism or its militarism. He couldn't blame the whole thing on me. It wasn't right. It just wasn't fair, and I couldn't handle it.

Hell, I'd given him a job when no one else would, a chance to earn a few bucks if we were lucky. And we had been! He could have fished with me for years, and there was an outside chance that he could have gotten his own boat one day. So why did he want to kill me? Wasn't it enough I'd lost my goddamn arm over there? What more did he want from me? Sure, I went. But I had had no choice. Going to Canada or to prison was too much to ask of an eighteen-year-old who'd always done what his father had told him.

Peering at the pages of his book in the dim light of the swaying boat, Tu must have felt like he was back in the tunnels with the ground heaving as the B-52's performed their nightly task. But he paid no mind to the roll of the sea or me and went on trying to decipher the will of heaven and the American way.

I stood there bracing myself against the nook, staring at him. "Tu."

He looked at me, eye level from the top berth, unstartled, his face clear and open yet distant and detached, impervious to whatever might happen.

"What are you reading tonight?"

"Thomas Jefferson."

I nodded. "Look, I'm sorry about what happened. I've been feeling kinda weird lately. And . . . well, I didn't mean nothin' by it."

He looked into me without the least change in his expression, as if he hadn't heard, didn't understand, or didn't care.

"Look," I said, going to my locker and removing the coffee. "I was just being crazy. I mean . . . I don't know what I was thinking." I lowered myself to the seat in the nook facing him.

Still he said nothing.

"What do you want me to say, goddamn it? I'm sorry about Vietnam, about what happened. I couldn't help it. I know what we did was wrong, but it wasn't my fault!" I was almost shouting as we swayed back and forth, staring into each other's eyes in the dim light. "Do you have any idea what it was like for me?"

"I think it cannot be easy. You were a young man. You did what your country says, and you are badly wounded. Your country ignores you. I am not blind. Your place and mine not so different. I not blame you for what happened in Vietnam. American government is to blame, but the people give government power, and they can, sometimes must, take it away. It is as Thomas Jefferson said.''

Now the son of a bitch had Jefferson on his side. It was a no-win situation. I went back up to the wheelhouse and drank for a while between coughing bouts. A few beers later I flipped on the radar and, seeing that there was not another boat close to us, I went below and crawled into my berth.

23
CHAPTER

I woke with a hangover. It was a miserable, gray, rainy day. The wind had dropped slightly, but was still blowing hard enough to knock the tops off the waves. The weather report called for conditions to improve.

As soon as I finished eating I broke out in a cold sweat. I went out on deck and threw up. My first shared meal with Tu in five days and I was immediately sick. I went below and lay down. How much later I woke I don't know, but I was drenched in sweat and felt little better.

I dragged myself up the companionway and stood in the shadows of the wheelhouse looking out at Tu. He was waist-deep in the trolling pit, his yellow slicker on, Mariners cap pulled low, head down, cigarette wedged in the corner of his mouth. The little bastard looked like he owned the boat. Probably thought he would soon.

A score of medium-size salmon lay gutted on the deck beside

him. I envisioned Tu gutted and sprawled on the deck. I reached for the rifle, chambered a round, and stepped to the doorway. Sighting down the barrel I flipped off the safety. Tu wavered in my sights as the deck rolled and my aim trembled.

Vietnam had seldom allowed a clear shot at the enemy. In the bush we fired at ghosts, but not before they wounded us. Sometimes from the air we caught the little bastards in the open, running through the paddies, and we made them dance to our tune. Better still was open season in the villages. Guilt by association. If you were there you were dead. That was the policy.

I killed a woman once. And the bundle she was clutching? I don't know about that, don't want to. She ran from her burning hooch into the line of fire. I saw her go down, both halves, the bundle fumbled away. It was an enemy village. Free-fire zone. That was the policy.

I could feel my fingerprint scrape along the edge of the trigger. Tu, intent upon the hunt, did not realize he was the prey. It would be so easy; all I had to do was squeeze and my troubles would be over.

But I could not bring myself to do it. I lowered the muzzle and flipped on the safety.

I lunged across the heaving deck, rifle in hand. When Tu looked up and saw me approaching he fell to the bottom of the trolling pit. I knelt over him and peered into his face. He looked up at me, frightened but unyielding.

"You've been poisoning me, you bastard! Why, tell me why? I gave you a job, bought you clothes, got you started fishing. What is it you want? My boat? What? All that bullshit about not blaming me for what happened in Vietnam. I told you I was sorry, you son of a bitch." I screamed, "What more do you want from me? Why are you trying to kill me?"

"I not try and kill you, Cap'n Mike. It not so. I swear. Tu your friend, Cap'n Mike. I not try and harm you."

"You're lying! How could you be my friend after what I've done?" I struggled to my feet. Grasping the rifle barrel I raised it overhead like an ax. "I'm sorry!" I screamed. "I'm sorry!"

"No! Cap'n Mike . . . !"

I crashed the rifle down against the trolling cage, splintering the stock. "I'm sorry! I'm sorry!" I cried as I flailed the shattered weapon against the piping.

Tu clipped me at the knees, taking me to the deck, just as the shooting started. We clung to each other as large-bore rifle and shotgun fire tore into the boat. I could hear glass shatter and chunks of wood—wheelhouse and window frame—fly. It sounded like a small squad-size ambush. They poured it on us: hot and heavy, rapid fire. Bullets whistled overhead, richocheted, rang the gurdies, and splintered the wheelhouse.

We lay side by side with our cheeks pressed to the wet deck, breathing hard into each other's face, an arm and a hook draped across each other's back. And then the business end of a shotgun broke our field of vision. I could smell the deathful odor on its breath.

Suddenly Tu was being wrestled from my embrace. There were grunts and curses. A boot struck me in the small of the back and I lost my last handful of Tu's jacket. Then the gun barrel pressed my neck firmly to the deck and I conceded.

I could see nothing of what happened after that, although it was not hard to guess: piracy, abduction, possible execution. Tu had certainly gone from the pan to the fire, and I assumed I would be next.

"Come on!" someone yelled. The gun came away from my neck. Then I took another boot in the back. "Don't move."

For a moment I didn't. I heard an engine rev and a body thump as it hit the deck. I felt *Leigh Anne* shudder as she was jolted, I raised my head. A rifle shot tore into the deck and I fell back. I squeezed my eyes shut and lay perfectly still.

I heard the boats pull away. There were two of them: *Westerly* and another. I'd been able to see the tops of *Westerly*'s twin masts as I lay with my head on the deck. Most likely it had been the two deckhands who'd boarded *Leigh Anne,* with McGuire's delivering the kicks to my back.

I rose slowly to my knees, keeping low, surveying the near horizon. Finding that clear I grasped the trolling cage and slowly pulled myself up. There was not another boat to be seen.

Leigh Anne was badly wounded. The wheelhouse windows were shot out. Fist-size holes had been punched here and there, and smaller puncture wounds dotted the walls. Both the trolling poles were down in the water, busted and trying to tear loose from the cap rail. The gurdies had been smeared like a thumb through soft green clay.

The trolling poles demanded attention, but I ignored them and went to the wheelhouse. The inside had been trashed: glass lay strewn about as if a bomb had exploded. Charts and books were scattered everywhere. The depth-sounder was a goner. The barometer had seen its last millibar. But the only thing I cared about was the radar. I saw where a bullet had ripped through its viewing hood and my hopes sank; it was my only chance of finding *Westerly* and Tu. I pulled the hood away and saw to my vast relief that the screen was intact. I switched it on and within moments the reassuring green glow with its sweeping arm came dimly into view. I bent closer and there were the two blips I was praying for.

I stepped out of the wheelhouse and up onto the rail. I put a foot up to the sill of the shot-out port window and hoisted myself onto the roof. Grasping the mast I looked to port and saw a squat little troller I recognized as the *Miss Mary* slinking away, and beyond her, fading into the mist, the unmistakable silhouette of *Westerly*.

I scrambled down off the roof and into the wheelhouse. The Loran was still operational and I took a fix on *Westerly*. I now knew exactly were Tu was. What good it would do me was something else, but at least I knew that much. I quickly set about clearing away the trolling gear before it beat the hull to pieces.

The port side of the boat had taken the brunt of the damage, and that included the fishing gear. The port trolling pole was busted in half and ripped from its hinge on the rail. No longer supported by the poles, the fishing lines hung from the their blocks, a tangled mess. The port gurdies were out of commission, so I had no choice but to cut away the lines. A hundred or so feet of stainless line with a dozen spreads attached and a sixty-pound cannonball hanging off the end was a terrible expense to cut loose, but there was no choice. Times three it was even more painful, but it all got the deep six.

The starboard pole was down but intact. I managed to get it

up alongside the boat and bring it aboard. Then I set compulsively to bring in the starboard lines.

The trolling poles are what keep the lines separated, holding each one wider than the next. Once the poles are down, the lines are free to career around like Olympic hammer throws, twisting the lines into steel cable. Even with two hands it would have been an impossible task. I was just going through the motions, any motions, because I was overwhelmed by what had happened and my inability to do anything about it.

Belatedly I got around to pumping the bilge, and with profound disinterest found it dry. At least these latter-day pirates had had the courtesy not to shoot *Leigh Anne* in the ass, beneath her water line. I cleared away a bit of the mess in the wheelhouse, righted my stool, and took a seat before the radar screen. And there I sat, chain-smoking, dreaming of a video game in which I controlled the joystick of life. I set little spaceships and rockets zipping across the screen, blasting away at *Westerly,* exploding her in an electronic Armageddon.

What I quickly realized about this plan, other than its blatant fantasy nature, was that Tu would go the way of the bad guys: It was a nondiscretionary cataclysm. I had another cigarette and pondered my predicament. What was needed was a flying saucer, one that could hover above *Westerly,* extract Tu, and then blow it to hell. That settled I went out on the deck, opened the fishhold, and lowered myself in. There I found the six-pack of beer I was looking for.

I was exhausted, bewildered. Was Tu poisoning me? If so, why had he knocked me to the deck when the shooting started? But if he wasn't poisoning me, why was I sick? The last time I'd vomited I'd seen blood. And I was coughing like a coal miner. My appetite was terrible, and I was constantly tired.

The twin blips, hovering in the outer circle, faded in and out as the the radar arm swept across them. What did McGuire intend to do? Surely he wouldn't kill Tu. I just couldn't bring myself to believe that. Even if my tortured logic had brought me to the brink of such an act, I didn't believe McGuire capable of it. And it was to his credit; I wasn't selling him short on guts—maybe brains, but not guts. He just wasn't a killer. But I, on the other hand . . .

So, what would he do? Make Tu walk the plank? Keelhaul him? Hold him ransom? Piracy and kidnapping were federal crimes. I could have Elliot Ness breathing down his neck in no time. But McGuire knew I wouldn't call in the Feds as surely as I knew he wouldn't kill Tu. So there it was, sort of a stand-off. As long as he didn't hurt Tu, he knew I wouldn't go to the cops, and since I knew he wouldn't, I didn't.

Undoubtedly McGuire was sitting at his radar screen that very moment, looking at my electronic image, thinking the same things I was, if with a somewhat different twist. He would put Tu ashore eventually, and the message would be clear: "I could have hurt him, even killed him, and next time I will. I am king of the fishing grounds. My word is law." And he would be right.

CHAPTER 24

As the afternoon wore on my anger grew with it. My one prize possession in all the world, my home, my livelihood, my love, *Leigh Anne* was in a shambles around my feet. And there, right there on the goddamn radar screen, was the man responsible! And I could not get to him.

Leigh Anne was not dead in the water—she could make it to port—but I'd have as soon scuttled her as turn tail and let Pete McGuire have his way. Still, I could not pursue *Westerly;* she had a longer range than *Leigh Anne,* and McGuire would just keep moving away.

Sly Stanislaus! That's who I needed: the Coast Guard. Sly could fly out, pick me up, and lower me onto *Westerly*'s deck. Simple. Just like the video games. But this was the real world, the arcade I seemed to function least well in. One didn't just dial the cavalry, or Pop. I'd have to do it on my own, or it wouldn't get done.

But I wanted to sleep, and without a moment's hesitation I

could have put my head down and done so. However, the game was over if I did. I might never wake up, or when I did the blips on my video screen would be scattered and I would never find Tu, never redeem myself.

My eyes went to the skiff lashed atop the trolling cage. I saw myself bobbing along in the dark through tall waves, and I shuddered. It was a six-foot rowboat, just the thing for getting from *Leigh Anne* to the dock when I was anchored out. Beneath it, mounted on the cage, was the little Seagull outboard I used to power it.

McGuire was less than a mile away. I could sneak in under his radar, board *Westerly,* slit his throat or cut off his balls, then call Alan and have him pick Tu and me up.

I lifted the mike from the CB and hailed *Talisman.* Alan and I had a prearranged code and frequency that we'd used since we first fished together; it was the only way we could talk to each other without letting the entire fleet listen in.

"Slomo, this is Iron Mike. Switching."

I repeated our code then tuned to our channel. If he was down on the compass rose—an area at the far side of the Prairie, obscured on the chart by a compass rose—then he might be out of range. Sometimes he could hear me though, when he was too far away for his weaker signal to carry, in which case he'd call me on the VHF. But my VHF was little more than an exploded shell with dangling wires and a twisted bracket.

Dead static. Or did I hear a break? Was Alan trying to punch through? Or was I hallucinating? I dialed the open frequency and tried again. Maybe he was in the hold icing down and hadn't heard me (Lois might not tell him if she had). Or maybe he was into a pocket and didn't want to quit it.

"Slomo, Slomo, this is Iron Mike. Got trouble. Got trouble. Switching."

I went over again, but still nothing.

So, there it was. No Alan. No cavalry. No Pop. Jus' me, boss. Jus' me.

Again I pondered sleep. It was almost dark. How easy it would be to succumb to my own moral indolence. I had once read that comedy was when the fool fell, and that tragedy was when the hero did. If I was going to take a fall, and surely I was, then all that remained of the illusion of choice was the direction in which I went down.

The deck was still doing a lively dance, and I about crushed myself when the skiff came off its overhead perch. Lying at my feet it looked impossibly small. The single oar lashed to the seat added little to encourage me. If the engine failed—presuming it started—I wasn't sure I could scull any better than to keep the bow into the swells.

Quickly I cleaned the spark plug—scraped it and gapped it with my switchblade—then filled the small tank with fresh fuel and bled the line. Then I slipped her over the side. Below deck I gathered my survival suit, hand compass, and signal flares. I made a sandwich and filled a bottle with water. In the wheelhouse I pocketed an extra pack of smokes, the flashlight, and took a final fix on *Westerly*. I set my pocket compass and tried to raise *Talisman* one last time.

"Slomo, this is Iron Mike. Switching."

And then, as if we earthlings had finally received a reply to our messages broadcast to the edge of the universe, I heard a faint voice whisper across the airwaves.

"Mike. Alan here. Read you loud and clear. How me?"

"Alan! Hot damn! I read you, brother. You're weak, but I read you. Where are you?"

"I got your message. I pulled the gear, and we're heading your way. You still up there where you caught that hump of fish?"

"Affirmative. Listen, Alan, I got big trouble. McGuire kidnapped Tu and shot up *Leigh Anne*. I'm taking the skiff and boarding *Westerly*. I need you to come get us off."

"That right? Well, why don't you wait for me? We'll go together."

"That's a negative. I'm doin' this one alone. But I'll need you to pick me up. Head for *Westerly*. When you find her lay off until I signal you."

"Okay. If you're sure you don't want to wait for me."

"I'm sure." I gave him *Westerly*'s Loran coordinates and signed off. Then I switched *Leigh Anne*'s running lights on and slid the wheelhouse door closed behind me.

I was as prepared as possible; I'd done everything short of

blackening my face. In my favor were the light winds, low visibility—clouds obscured the moon—and the element of surprise. Against me were the size of the swells, the size of my boat, the low visibility—it was not easy to know where I was going—and the absurdity of what I was doing. The Seagull came immediately to life, and my commando operation was under way.

The swells were not steep, not breaking, but down in the trough I could see nothing, and coming up over the crest I could see scarcely more. I had long ago rigged the outboard's throttle with a ring to slip the hook through so I could drive with a free hand. Head down, I peered into the dully luminescent dial of the compass. The skiff scooted down the back sides of the swells, slowly climbing their faces, the Seagull whining in my ear. I could not correlate the compass heading with the distant lights I saw as I rose over the crests of the waves. Nor did they appear to be coming closer as time, and fuel, wore on.

If I missed *Westerly* I was doomed; I'd never find my way back to *Leigh Anne*.

The sea broke beside me, bringing me out of the trance I had slipped into. It spoke of whales, sea serpents, cold water, drowning, death. If I was dying, then I reckoned that doing so in the name of something decent would be a sight better than some of the other ways I'd almost died, and probably should have. I no longer cared if Tu was trying to kill me (certainly my judgment was suspect, that much I knew, but whether he was made little difference). If he didn't have the right to kill me, he surely had every reason to. Still, I could repair none of the damage that I and my country had done to him and his. I could, however, see to it that he had a fighting chance to make it in his new home, and that the likes of Pete McGuire kept their goddamn hands off him. That much I could do.

I hung the compass around my neck by its lanyard and leaned into the bow for the water bottle. I took a swig and when I came up over the next crest saw that the boat lights in the distance were noticeably closer. Soon I was able to take a sighting and see that the boat I was slowly closing in on lay near enough to my original heading for me to think that it might be *Westerly*.

Suddenly, a painting that I had seen as a child, of a black

man adrift on the high sea in a small dismantled boat, loomed before me. On the horizon, going away, was a steam ship. The man leaned against the rail of his boat without a look to the ship, his legs comfortably outstretched. He may not have noticed the ship's passage, although he could just as easily have seen it and turned away, knowing he could do nothing to gain his rescue.

I assumed it was one of those human condition paintings: the solitariness of man, the futility of salvation. Regardless, I always took solace from that painting. Despite the seemingly hopelessness of the situation, I always knew he'd make it, somehow, despite the odds.

As I came up over the top of another swell I saw that it was indeed *Westerly* I had been bearing down on. Having pinpointed my destination, my desire to arrive unannounced became paramount. The goddamn engine was like a chain saw at the end of my arm. If I hadn't been downwind of *Westerly*, McGuire would have been up on deck sending cannon shot across my bow, even at this distance. I'd have to kill the engine before I got too close. And I'd have a devil of a time skulling my one oar off the stern of this little skiff and making any headway. My only chance was to get above *Westerly* and drift down to her. I adjusted my heading.

No longer heading into the waves, the skiff rolled side to side as well as up and down. And the bile that festered within me began to boil. My skin crawled beneath the layers of wool shirts and sweaters and rubberized outerwear. I went cold. My stomach tightened. The boat pitched and a cresting wave pelted me with liquid BB shot. Moments later I was heaving in the bottom of the boat.

I held my course until I was sure I'd pass out, then I brought the bow back into the sea. Immediately I felt better, but I had precious little resolve to go on.

Any desire to do the *right* thing had washed overboard. No abstract sense of justice lingered. Only anger remained. I'd been overflowing with anger all my adult life, but no one would recognize it. My anger and rage were ignored, denied. But the more my anger was denied the angrier I became. "If you or any of your party should be discovered we will disavow all knowledge of you. Good-bye and good luck.''

But it was neither free-floating anger nor abstract hostility. I'd been fucked over. Screwed royally. Lied to by my country, my government, and my parents. The very precepts that I had grown up on—honesty, dignity, respect for life, the importance of being a good human being—had all been picked off one by one like clay pipes in a shooting gallery. They were hollow shells, Styrofoam, and papier-mâché on a movable landscape. I had nothing to build my world on. I was adrift in a liquid world without a life jacket.

The question was: Why hadn't I drowned long ago? Why hadn't I held myself under? Why had I survived Vietnam when so many had died? And why did I survive still when so many could not, would not?

CHAPTER

When finally I killed the Seagull it seemed as if I had been isolated within the whine of the small outboard forever. Abruptly the shell was broken and I was surrounded by the surge of the sea and the breadth of the sky. I was at once euphoric, exhausted, adrenaline-pumped, on the edge of death, and completely alive. I drifted down on *Westerly* in darkness. Only her running lights, high overhead, faintly glowed.

Old converted schooner that she was, *Westerly* had a lot of freeboard—the height from her waterline to deck—and presented a formidable castle wall that I would have to scale. There would be no inside help on this one, no fair maiden to lower the drawbridge. My entrance could be nothing short of acrobatic; anything less would result in failure.

Swells that *Westerly* ignored had me riding up and down beside her as if I were trapped in a goddamn dumbwaiter. Slowly I worked my way aft to her high, rounded transom. Here the waterline cut in beneath her slightly overhanging stern, and I could get up beside her without smacking the skiff against the hull. With flashlight, flares, and knife securely in my pockets, I took the bowline from the skiff between my teeth and stood slowly on the seat.

Immediately I was a drunk on a tightrope. The first swell tried unsuccessfully to catapult me into the sea. Fighting for my balance I barely managed not to dash the skiff against the hull. When the next swell lifted me I lunged for *Westerly*'s deck, and there I hung: hook embedded in the rail, skiff gone out from under me, legs and free arm flailing for a purchase.

For a moment I swung from the point of my hook as if I were gimbaled. The belts that secured the medieval device to my arm cut into my shoulder and chest. I began to slip. The sea licked my boots. Finally, I had to stop fighting my momentum and give in to it. Swinging wide enough to grab hold of the backstay—running down from the mast to the rail—I threw a leg up over and rolled onto the deck with a thud.

I rummaged quickly through my pockets for the switchblade, as I expected McGuire and his deckhand to be on me in a flash. Hook at the end of one arm, knife at the end of the other, bowline still clenched between my teeth, I backed against the rail and waited. But as the seconds stuttered by, with no sign of the palace guard rousing, a smile curled steadily at the corners of my mouth. In the dark of night, in a pathetically small craft, I had crossed almost a mile of open ocean with a sizable swell running to board unobserved the enemy vessel. I stifled a laugh that grew into a hacking cough I could not contain.

I turned down on the deck and buried my face in the crook of an arm and the palm of my hand. I gasped for air and forced myself to stop breathing, stop coughing. The moment passed, taking with it my self-congratulatory mood. In thirty seconds I had almost undone what it had taken me more than two hours to accomplish.

I lay quietly on the deck but heard nothing save the wind steady in McGuire's rigging and my own heart beating in my ears. I rose slowly to my knees and tied off the skiff to the backstay. She trailed away in the wind and swells and would not give away my presence by tapping on the hull.

Surprise was paramount. Without it someone would be hurt,

seriously hurt. And while my intentions toward McGuire and his deckhand remained unclear, I was perfectly clear regarding my own desire not to be hurt.

I wanted the situation resolved in such a way that Tu and I would never be fucked with again. Not necessarily because we had beaten the opposition into submission, but because we had demonstrated that the cost of doing battle with us was too high. Which is exactly what the United States had finally concluded in Vietnam.

I slipped out of my cumbersome foul-weather gear and cautiously approached the wheelhouse. I slid back the door and slipped in. It was warm and the faint glow of the radar screen seeped from its conical viewing hood. I pressed my face to the opening and there I was: *X* marks the spot. *Leigh Anne* was in the same position relative to McGuire's screen as *Westerly* had been in mine. But McGuire or his deckhand had rudely put an *X* across *Leigh Anne*'s silhouette.

They had evidently spent the day as I had: sitting before their radar screen, watching my position, ready to keep their distance should I come for Tu. But hours later, with no discernable movement on my part and night well on, they had apparently called it a victory and gone to bed. Or so the legions of empty beer cans led me to believe, although the fact of the radar remaining at its vigil hinted as much at caution as drunken neglect.

I had never been aboard *Westerly* before, but I had seen that her fo'c'sle had a separate entry up front, and that she had a large fishhold amidships. I assumed that the galley and captain's cabin were below me, at the bottom of the darkened companionway I stood peering into. It was doubtful that a passage below deck connected galley and fo'c'sle.

Tu would either be forward, bound in solitary, or below. If he was forward in the fo'c'sle, then I would find McGuire and his deckhand at the foot of the companionway. Maybe they'd seen me approach, heard me come aboard, even watched with amusement as I writhed on the deck. And turning from the radar they'd retreated below deck, where they awaited me.

I went instantly cold with the sudden realization that the *X* I'd seen over *Leigh Anne* on the radar screen had to have been made within minutes—ten, fifteen at the most—as the position of the two boats was constantly changing.

I turned quickly back to the screen. It was as I belatedly surmised; *Leigh Anne*'s radar image was just beginning to drift off her mark. As I raised my face from the viewing cone I heard a foot fall and then a burst of light blinded me.

I dropped to the floor and slid to the head of the companionway. I could feel the cold breath of panic, like a lonely drowning. I squeezed tight the trembling knife and forced my back up against the side of the counter and my eyes to the edge of the window. A glowing cigarette tip approached the wheelhouse.

Halfway down, *Westerly*'s companionway turned sharply to the left. I was around the corner when the door slid back and footsteps entered the wheelhouse. Below me a dimly lit passageway showed nothing, and no sound hinted at what I would find when I plunged down the final steps.

Above, in the wheelhouse, a beer can was lifted, first one and then another and another. Each was set down sharply, their emptiness sounding loudly in the darkness. "Shit," a voice muttered.

When I hit the passageway I came face to face with Tu. He was sitting quietly at the galley table and was obviously shocked to see me. His mouth fell open but no words came forth. I spun around. Behind me the empty passageway led to a darkened doorway. Footsteps descended the stairs. I stepped quickly into the galley, desperate for a place to hide. Tu, arms and legs bound at his side, motioned with his head that I should slide in beneath the table. I wedged myself into the corner behind his legs.

The footsteps made the bottom of the companionway and turned into the galley without a word to Tu. From the knees down, I could see that it was the deckhand as he bent to the cooler and searched out a beer. The legs were long and thin, just the opposite of his captain's.

He must have marked *Leigh Anne*'s position on the screen and gone below to his quarters for cigarettes or matches—something—just as I was lunging for *Westerly*'s stern. I had underestimated their vigilance, while they had given me more and less credit than I deserved. More by thinking I'd do anything; less by not fully realizing the extent to which I'd go if I did.

The deckhand stepped to the table and jostled Tu, checking the ropes that bound him, but fortunately didn't check the ones around his ankles.

"Looks like your skipper ain't comin' for you, Chinaman."

"Vietnamese," Tu said defiantly.

"What's the difference?" His beer popped open. "You're still a slope. And he still ain't comin' for you. Sleep tight, Chinaman." He stepped away from the table and mounted the companionway.

I quickly cut the ropes from Tu's legs and crawled out from beneath the table.

"Where's McGuire?" I whispered, still on my hands and knees.

Tu nodded down the passageway.

"Okay. Stay put. Don't move. If he comes out I want him to think you're still tied up."

"I am."

I crawled quietly to the foot of the companionway and listened. When I heard the wheelhouse door open and then shut I got to my feet and took the stairs two at a time. Out on deck I spied him taking a last wizz over the side.

His business finished, he disappeared down the forward companionway, sliding the hatch closed as he went. Following quickly on his heels, I fastened the hasp over the latch and slipped the peg in.

Back in the wheelhouse I turned on the radar. It came quickly to life. There was *Leigh Anne,* still farther off the X but holding position. What the deckhand had failed to notice before retiring was the new blip that had just sailed onto the screen from the opposite compass heading.

I turned on McGuire's Loran. It was the same make as mine but a newer model, and it took me a few minutes before I could work out *Westerly* and *Talisman*'s coordinates. When finally I did I flipped on the CB, switched channels, and turned the volume down.

"Slomo, this is Iron Mike," I whispered.

Then I gave him the two sets of coordinates and asked him

to conform by breaking squelch twice. Moments later the static on the channel was interrupted once and then again. It was a technique we'd used in Vietnam when the enemy had been breathing down our necks. I instructed Alan to approach to within one hundred meters then hold his position until we signaled.

I found Tu as before, calmly sitting at the table, arms bound at his sides. I sat beside him and cut away the ropes. As soon as he was free he wanted to be gone. I put up my hand and shook my head. I explained the necessity of saying good-bye to McGuire. At first he was disinclined to have anything further to do with him. But when I explained the situation to him in greater detail—the deckhand's confinement, Alan's approach—he heartily nodded his agreement.

What to do? That was the question. Disarm him would certainly be the first thing, but then what? I wasn't going to kill him. The nauseating panic I'd felt in the wheelhouse had reminded me all too clearly of the terror I'd experienced in the war: the horror of pending death, mine or someone else's. I'd killed enough, been violent enough. I felt as if I'd lived my life by the gun, or the hook. The brain-of-the-dog growled for blood, quick and savage. The opportunity was at hand, but I'd had enough. I wasn't about to turn into Mr. Mellow, but the brain-of-the-dog could be fed a new diet, appeased with wit rather than brute force.

I tapped the tip of the switchblade on the table top. What to do?

Fixed to the hull at the end to the table was a small wire corral containing salt, pepper, and catsup. For no particular reason it occurred to me that McGuire was probably one of those people who put catsup on his eggs. The thought stuck with me, showed me just the thing. I'd promised him I'd cut off his balls if he fucked with me, and that's exactly what I'd do. Well, almost. I'd put catsup on his eggs!

I removed the catsup bottle from the holder and laid a thick red line of sauce along the edge of the knife blade. I smiled knowing that Tu's disciplined nature would not allow him to ask what his curiosity was dying to know. Then I placed the switchblade in the middle of the table and whispered my instructions into his ear. Laughter puffed his cheeks, and I had to put my hand to his mouth quickly before his merriment escaped.

Together we tiptoed down the passageway to McGuire's cabin. It was a small room, taken up mostly by his double berth. We could see him clearly from the door. Stripped to his skivvies, half in and half out of his covers, he displayed the unconscious vulnerability of the sleeping.

I stole into the room and returned with his rifle. Now it was Tu's turn. Catsup in hand, he stepped up beside the berth. Cautiously he reached for the waistband of McGuire's shorts. If he woke now it'd just be a slug fest. McGuire would take the brunt of it, but then he'd be even more of a bear. What we wanted were his claws. McGuire turned, and Tu fell back.

I raised the rifle to McGuire's sleeping form. How easy it would be to rid myself of my archenemy. One shot and all my troubles would be . . . over? There was something disturbingly familiar with that line of thought. Hadn't I had those same thoughts about Tu, just today, when I'd come close to shooting him? I lowered the rifle and leaned it against the wall.

Tu motioned me to come alongside him and take the catsup bottle. Leaning forward, one arm extended, he lay his forefinger on McGuire's brow. Ever so gently Tu traced a tiny circle just above the bridge of McGuire's nose. For a moment his hand rose toward his face, but then it fell back. Like a reptile with its belly being stroked, he moved not a muscle. Cautiously, while Tu continued to massage his forehead, I hiked his waistband and anointed his genitals with a large dollop of catsup.

Dastardly deed accomplished, we retreated to the galley. I set the rifle in the companionway and had Tu sit at the table as if he were still bound. Before him lay the open knife with the catsup-covered blade. Here was the central prop of our guerrilla theater; it needed to be sprung on the audience at precisely the right moment. I went to the sink and tore off a section of paper towel, had Tu fold it into a tent and place it over the knife.

Then I pulled a flare from my pocket and showed it to him. His eyes bugged. Maybe he thought it was high explosive. I laughed out loud. With the hook I pried the cap off the end. It came to life with a pop, smoking and spewing, red and white flames shooting from the end. I tossed it into McGuire's cabin and stepped up into the companionway.

Within seconds McGuire came screaming out of his sleep. I could hear him dancing about the deck, swearing at the top of his lungs. Torch in hand, he ran past me to the table where Tu calmly sat.

"You scum-suckin' motherfuckin' son of a bitch. What the hell's goin' on?" McGuire was beside himself. Screaming, hopping mad, he couldn't curse fast enough to keep up with his agitation.

Tu sat motionless, unruffled. "We're havin' some kinda fun now, hey, Cap'n McGuire," he said straight-faced, then broke into a broad grin.

McGuire started to turn to see whom Tu was sharing his amusement with, but I put the rifle firmly to the back of his head, and he stood very still.

"Morning, Pete. No, don't bother turnin' around. I look the same as when you last saw me. Except you had the gun then, and I was face down on my deck. Remember that?" When he didn't answer I tapped the barrel of the rifle against his skull like a pool stick against the cue ball. "Remember?"

"I remember," he said defiantly.

"Good. Wouldn't want you to forget what brings us together this morning. Tu, now that we've got Pete's attention, why don't you take that flare up on deck. Wave it over your head and then throw it overboard."

Tu removed the flare from McGuire's hand without question and disappeared up the companionway. The galley darkened to the dim glow of the single overhead light. Moments later Tu returned with a nod and resumed his seat. I tossed him the flashlight.

"Sorry to have to do this to you, Pete, but remember what I said I'd do to you if you didn't stop fucking with me?"

He flinched. The hook was baited. Now all he had to do was take it.

"Remember?"

"I remember. I remember."

I nodded. Tu whipped the paper tent from the knife and turned the flashlight on it. He held the beam on the blade just long enough for McGuire to have a flash of recognition, but not long enough to decipher fully what he'd seen.

Then I took the hook to McGuire's waistband and pulled his shorts down around his knees. He thought to resist, but I tapped his skull again with the rifle barrel and he held fast. I stepped to Tu's side. He switched on the flashlight once more. This time the beam fell on McGuire's groin, illuminating the gooey red mess.

It was the first inkling he'd had that there was anything amiss at that precious juncture between his legs. His head dropped suddenly. Shooting his hands to his penis and balls he made a hasty examination. Then he rubbed his reddened fingers together and put them to his mouth. When the message sent to his brain by his tongue was finally interpreted, his facial expres-- sion changed swiftly from that of terror to one of relief.

There had been but a fleeting instant between vision and recognition. But that instant held volumes. And it began with the possibility that he'd been cut. He might have spit out the hook, but he'd bitten down, tasted blood, and had been seized with the knowledge that he'd almost been gutted. Once the moment had passed he tried to deny it. But we had been witness. And he saw that we had.

McGuire, the penitent, shorts around his knees, stood stunned, disbelieving. Tu, the presiding judge, sat straight-backed at the table, hands folded before him. I, the prosecutor, was almost at attention, the rifle across my chest at a modified present arms. There were no smirks of smug satisfaction on our side of the bench, only the steady gazes of the just on the vanquished.

I switched the rifle to my hooked arm and tapped the side of my head with a finger. "Right here, Pete. Right here is the only reason your nuts are hangin' between your legs and not flying from *Leigh Anne*'s mast. And don't forget it. Don't you ever forget it.

"Now, pull your shorts up; you look ridiculous."

CHAPTER 26

Dawn. *Leigh Anne* and *Talisman* drifted together in a calm sea. I was in a daze. Exhausted, exhilarated, slightly queasy in the stomach from lack of sleep and too much coffee, I stood with a foot up on *Talisman*'s gunnel, a cigarette burning, eyeballing the damage done my boat.

She was plenty busted up. No one-day repairs this time. We'd have to take her back to Everett. And it wouldn't look good, us coming home with the boat shot up. Word would get around. But once I started charging on McGuire's account at the local marine supply, that'd get around too.

It was an arrangement Pete and I had worked out in the wee hours of the morning. We had even put it in writing: He'd pay for the materials to refurbish *Leigh Anne*—including barometer, depth-finder, and VHF—Tu and I would donate our labor. That way Pete kept his balls, and, as a courtesy, we kept quiet. Only Tu and I—and a few close friends—would know of his near loss.

* * *

After confining Pete in the fo'c'sle with his deckhand—the hasp wasn't so strong that they couldn't break out—Tu and I had boarded *Talisman*. It was quite an emotional moment for him and me. I think Tu had fully expected that McGuire would execute him. And considering what I'd put him through in the days prior to his abduction, he had no reason to think that he might be rescued.

But he had. Through an act of supreme will and effort I had done just that. And at least as important, I had used my wits and not lost them. No one had been hurt, only a little catsup had been shed, and Tu was safe. I felt vindicated.

Nothing would ever make up for the blood, real and imagined, that I had shed in Vietnam, but I had allowed no more to be spilled on my watch.

Tu and I stood silently beside each other as *Westerly* receded in the first light of dawn. Then we began to laugh. We looked at each other and our laughter crisscrossed the maze of distrust, animosity, and sorrow that bound us together as surely as it held us apart. For a moment my laughter turned to tears. Awkwardly we threw our arms across each other's shoulders. Then I began to laugh again, uproarious cosmic tickle laughter! We hugged, slapped backs, danced a jig. We had won! McGuire would never fuck with us again.

Lois came up on deck toting a pan of dirty dishes.

"Best meal I've eaten in a long time," I said of the pancakes, bacon, and coffee she'd whipped up shortly after we'd found *Leigh Anne*.

"Thanks."

Flattery wouldn't get me far with her.

"I don't suppose you can do dishes with one hand?" she said more as a statement than a question.

I smiled, raised the hook.

She drew up a bucket of sea water and doused the dishes she'd set on the hatch cover. Her soft gentle face was weary from the long night. A thick braid hung down over one shoulder as she bent to her work. She wore a dark hand-knitted wool sweater, jeans, and, as always, her thongs.

"Tu's funny," Lois laughed, looking up at me. "He was telling Alan what you guys did to McGuire, but he was too embarrassed to go into detail in front of me, even though you'd already spelled it out graphically."

"Dignity. That's what Tu has. Extraordinary dignity. On *Westerly,* while I was hiding under the table, beneath his legs, he was arguing with McGuire's deckhand that he's Vietnamese, not Chinese." I inhaled on my cigarette then shook my head. "You may not believe this, but for a while I actually thought Tu was trying to kill me."

Her expression turned incredulous. "Why shouldn't I believe that? You used to think the same thing of Leigh Anne."

"Did I?" I inhaled again and started coughing.

"Anyway, I don't know why you're so worried about other people trying to kill you when you're doing such a good job of it yourself."

I grinned, pitched the butt into the sea. "You never did like me much, did you?"

She looked up at me again, surprised. "I thought it was the other way around."

"Really?"

"Yeah. I never disliked you, Michael, I just liked Leigh Anne so much more. And I didn't think you were good for her." She paused to rinse her dishes. "Besides, I never understood your relationship. She loved you, I saw that much. And she told me that when you were first together you were wonderful to her. She knew it had to do with Vietnam, your weirdness, but she couldn't really figure it. I mean, it was obvious, you'd lost your arm, but there was so much more to it. She used to ask Alan and me about Vietnam, as if we could explain what had happened to you."

"Why'd she ask you?"

She fixed her gaze on me. "My brother was killed there. I thought you knew. Didn't Alan ever tell you?"

"No. I didn't know that. I'm sorry."

"Long time ago."

"Is it so easy to forget?"

"Easy? No." She shook her head. "But I was only ten when he died, and I didn't know him very well," she said sadly.

Lois had just the sort of connection with Vietnam that I wished Leigh Anne had had. Something less painful would have served: friend of a friend who'd died, a cousin who'd been wounded. Anything. Even if she'd been an antiwar protester. Just some way, however remotely, for her to have touched upon the horror. But Vietnam hadn't affected her life before I came along. It suddenly dawned on me that I'd *chosen* her for precisely that reason. And then I'd almost killed her because of it.

I sat down on the gunnel and rubbed my hand across my face. I started to reach for a cigarette then checked myself. "You ever hear from her?" I asked.

"Leigh Anne? We write."

"How's she doin'?"

"She's engaged," she replied cautiously.

"So I heard. I'm happy for her. I hope the guy falls and breaks his neck and she comes back to me. But I'm happy for her. Really."

"Really what?" she asked, hoisting her bucket of dishes and moving toward the wheelhouse. "Really hope her boyfriend breaks his neck, or really hope she's happy?"

I shrugged. "Both."

Half an hour later—with the four of us gathered on *Talisman*'s deck—we made our good-byes.

Tu was effusive in his praise of everyone. We had all done a superb job. The timing was flawless. We had taken the enemy completely by surprise and routed him. I could imagine him extolling his troops in much the same way after they'd sprung an ambush on an unsuspecting patrol. I was glad we were no longer on opposite sides. He pumped Alan's hand up and down. Then he half-bowed to Lois.

"Thanks, Alan." I extended my hand. We shook. He was tired, but he'd obviously enjoyed his part in the rescue.

"Quite a puller you got there," he said of Tu.

I watched Tu as he swung across onto *Leigh Anne*. "Yeah, we're quite the loose association."

"How's that?"

I shook my head. "You had to have been there. Anything you need from Everett? A new Loran? VHF? McGuire's paying."

We laughed.

"Look for us down around Westport when you get back," he said.

I nodded. "Guess you'll be glad to be closer to home?" I said to Lois, who was about to fall asleep leaning against Alan.

She nodded. "We'll have to have supper when we're all in port together."

"Tu and I would like that. Really."

Lois smiled. "Next time I write Leigh Anne I'll tell her you're happy for her."

I leaned forward and kissed her on the cheek. "Thanks."

We cast off and waved good-bye; then Tu and I set about straightening *Leigh Anne* away. Window glass littered the wheelhouse floor, as did chunks of wall, electronic components, and anything else that had gotten in the way of the barrage.

Despite our exhaustion, or perhaps because of it, Tu and I veritably whistled while we worked. Stepping about each other in the small wheelhouse as we swept and straightened, we were all grins. Bouts of laughter filled the cabin as bursts of gunfire had less than twenty-four hours before.

It all seemed something of a dream: my suspicions of Tu, the attack on *Leigh Anne,* my midnight skiff ride, the scene with McGuire.

"Some kinda fun we're having now, hey, Tu?"

"Some kinda fun, Cap'n Mike."

As we motored for home the morning slapped us in the face through the shot-out windows. Crisp and clear. The sea was dark, held a long gentle swell. The sky was a pale turquoise. There were clouds to the north, over Vancouver Island, and before us, clinging to the tops of the Olympics. Half a dozen trollers were already at it, their poles angled out, unseen lines sweeping beneath.